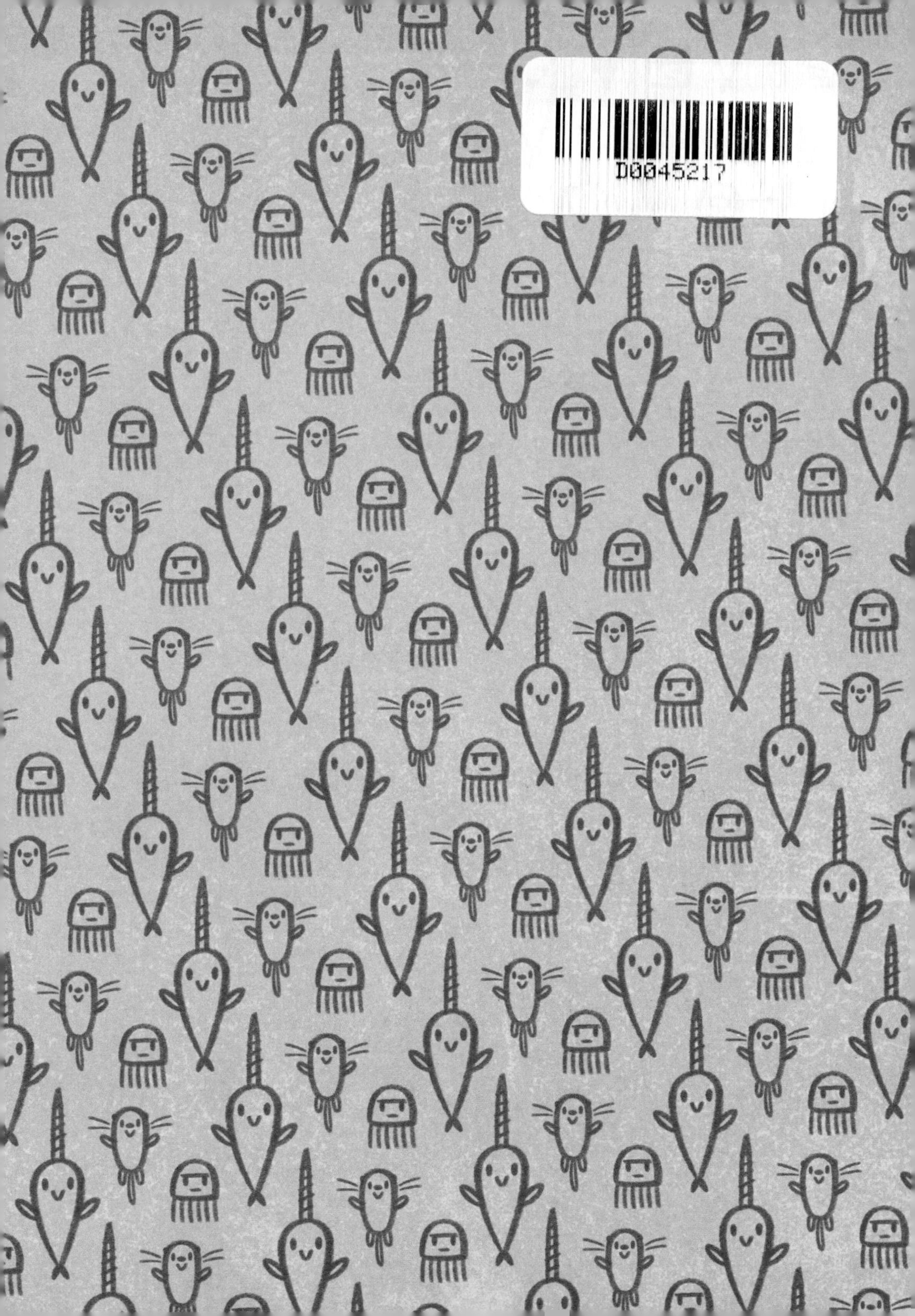

HAVE YOU READ THESE
NARWHAL AND JELLY BOOKS?

NARWHAL: UNICORN OF THE SEA!

SUPER NARWHAL AND JELLY JOLT

PEANUT BUTTER AND JELLY

NARWHAL'S
OTTER FRIEND

BEN CLANTON

tundra

TO THE OTTERLY AWESOME
TARA WALKER!

Text and illustrations copyright © 2019 by Ben Clanton

Tundra Books, an imprint of Penguin Random House Canada Young Readers, a Penguin Random House Company

Library and Archives Canada Cataloguing in Publication

Clanton, Ben, 1988–, author, illustrator
Narwhal's otter friend / Ben Clanton.

(A Narwhal and Jelly book ; 4)
Issued in print and electronic formats.
ISBN 978-0-7352-6248-5 (hardcover).—ISBN 978-0-7352-6250-8 (ebook)

I. Graphic novels. I. Title.

PZ7.C523Nar 2019   j813'.6   C2018-900681-I
                                           C2018-900682-X

Published simultaneously in the United States of America by Tundra Books of Northern New York, an imprint of Penguin Random House Canada Young Readers, a Penguin Random House Company

Library of Congress Control Number: 2018936944

Edited by Tara Walker and Jessica Burgess
Designed by Ben Clanton
The artwork in this book was rendered in colored pencil, watercolor and ink, and colored digitally.
The text was handlettered by Ben Clanton.

(map) © NYPL Digital Collections; (ice caps) © Maksimilian/Shutterstock; (large wave) © EpicStockMedia/Shutterstock; (small wave) © EpicStockMedia/Shutterstock; (waffle) © Tiger Images/Shutterstock; (strawberry) ©Valentina Razumova/Shutterstock; (pickle) © dominitsky/Shutterstock; (spoon) © Paul Burton/Thinkstock; (pot) © Devonyu/Thinkstock; (Earth [modified]) © NASA/NOAA GOES Project; (boom box) © valio84sl/Thinkstock; (brick) Stason4ic/Thinkstock

Species population and status information obtained from *The IUCN Red List of Threatened Species* as of time of printing.

Printed and bound in China

www.penguinrandomhouse.ca

5   6   7   23 22 21 20 19

CONTENTS

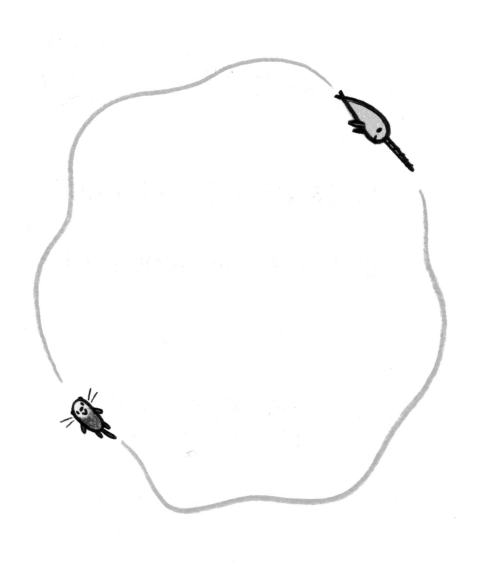

NARWHAL'S OTTER HALF?

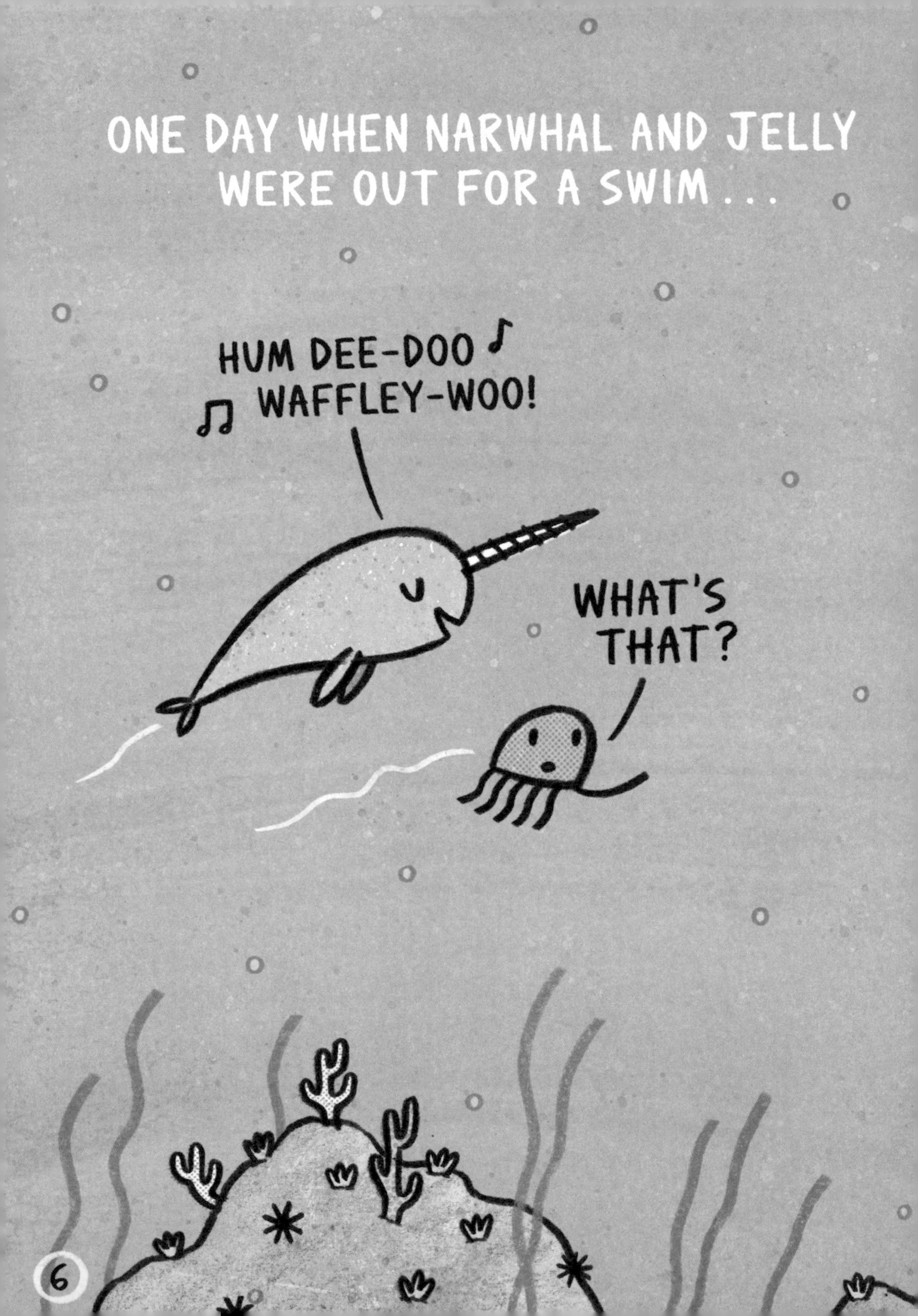
ONE DAY WHEN NARWHAL AND JELLY WERE OUT FOR A SWIM . . .
HUM DEE-DOO WAFFLEY-WOO!
WHAT'S THAT?

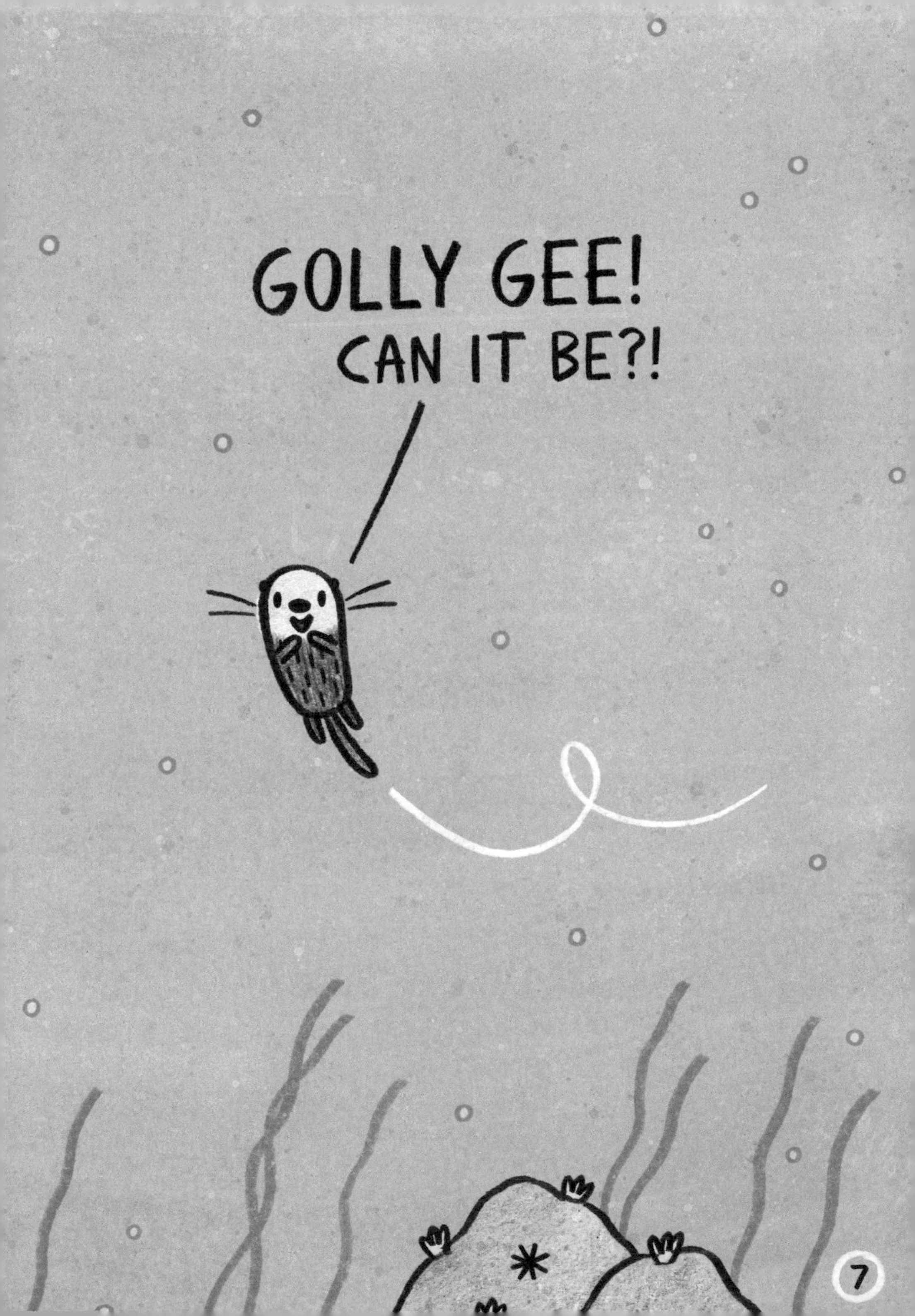
GOLLY GEE!
CAN IT BE?!

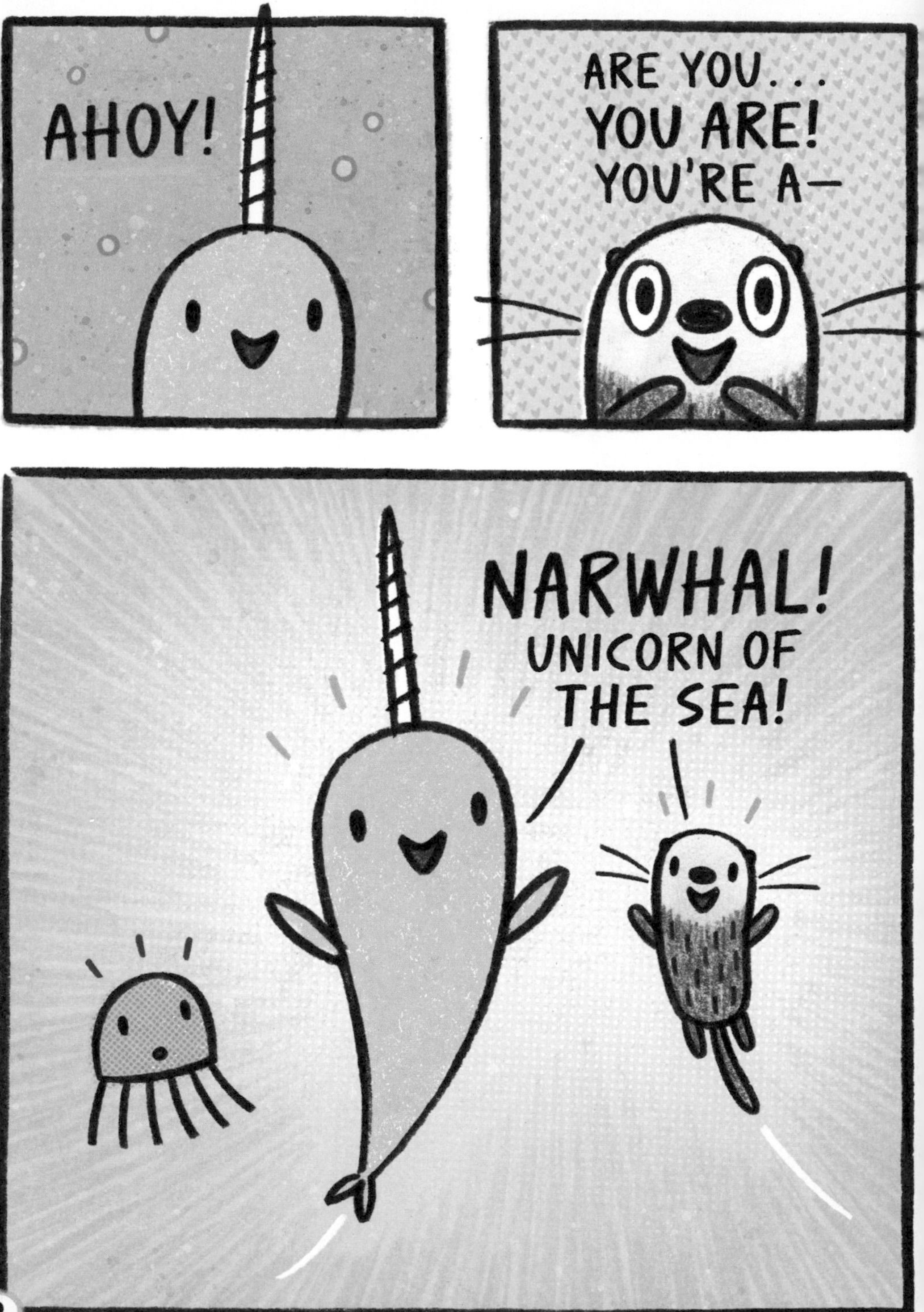
AHOY!
ARE YOU . . .
YOU ARE!
YOU'RE A—
NARWHAL!
UNICORN OF
THE SEA!

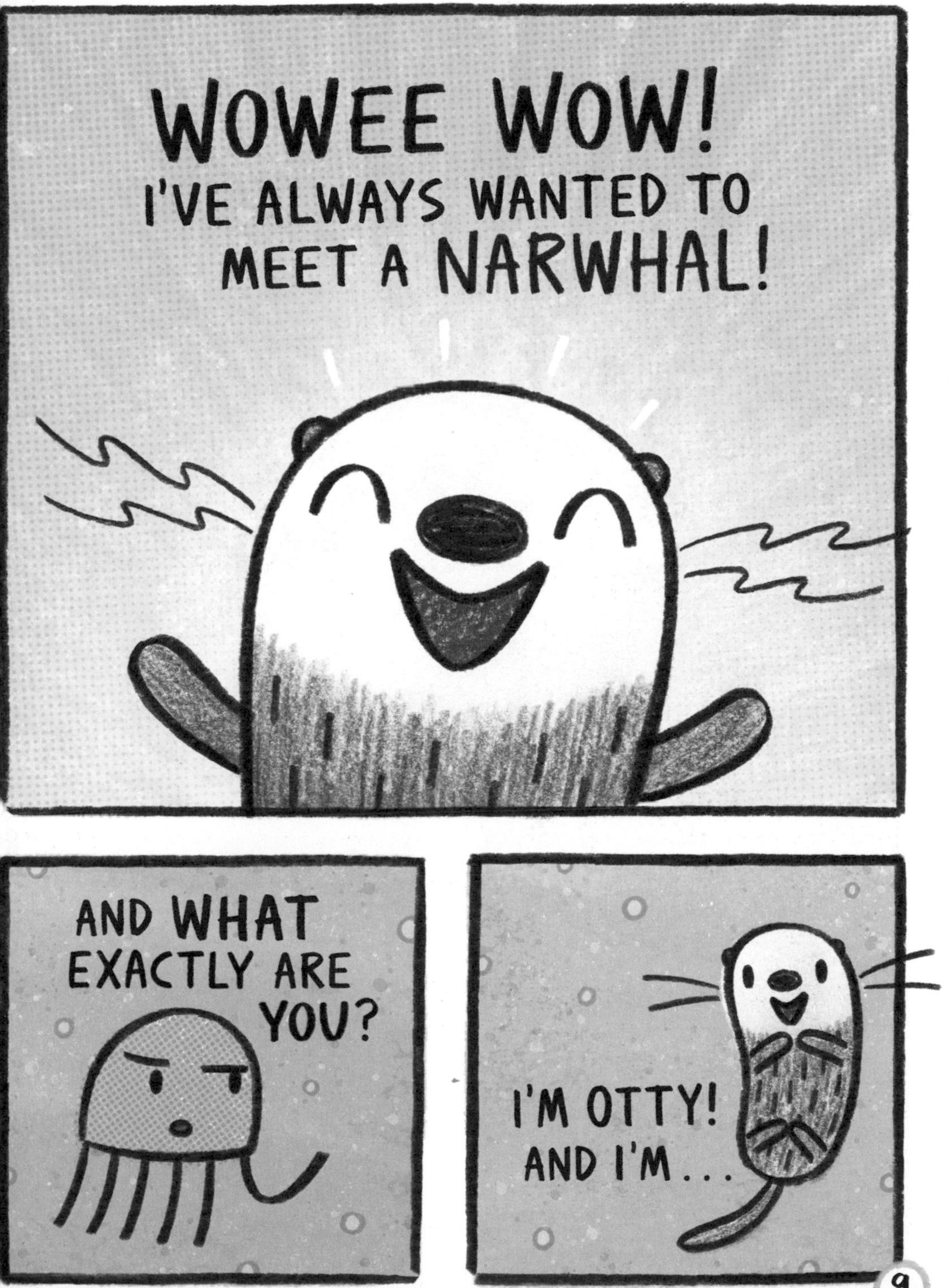
WOWEE WOW!
I'VE ALWAYS WANTED TO MEET A NARWHAL!
AND WHAT EXACTLY ARE YOU?
I'M OTTY!
AND I'M . . .

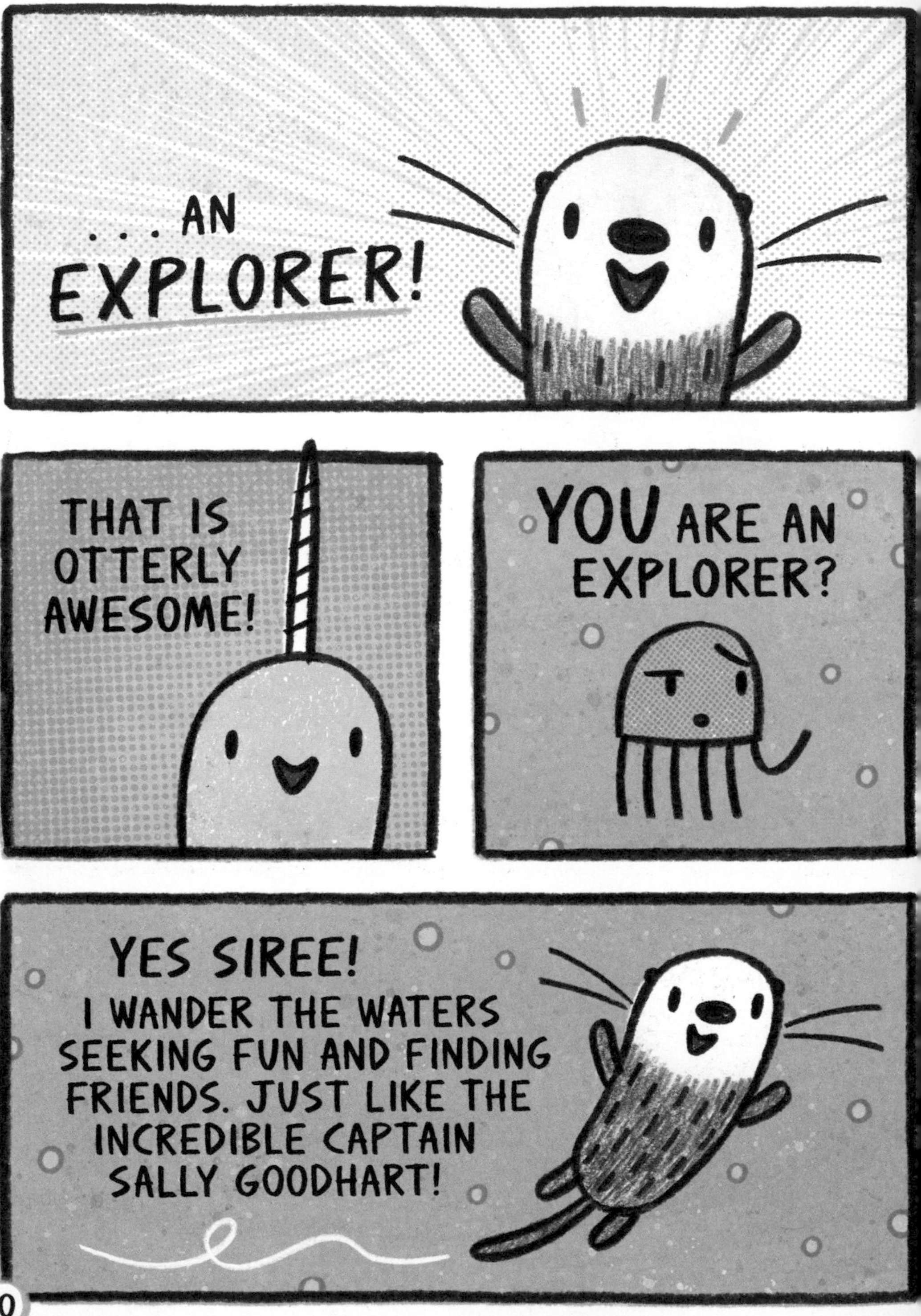
. . . AN EXPLORER!
THAT IS OTTERLY AWESOME!
YOU ARE AN EXPLORER?
YES SIREE!
I WANDER THE WATERS SEEKING FUN AND FINDING FRIENDS. JUST LIKE THE INCREDIBLE CAPTAIN SALLY GOODHART!

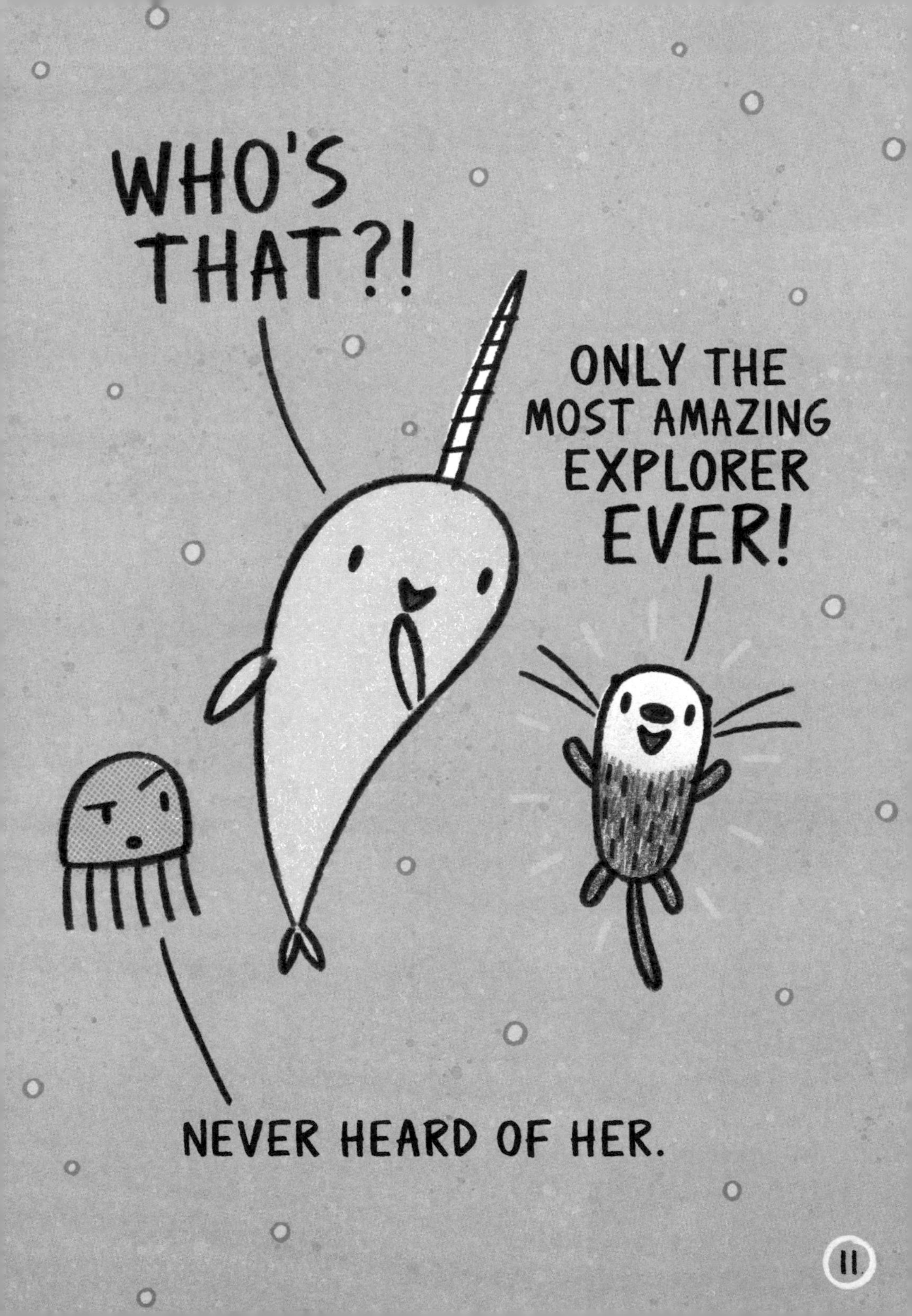
WHO'S THAT?!
ONLY THE MOST AMAZING EXPLORER EVER!
NEVER HEARD OF HER.

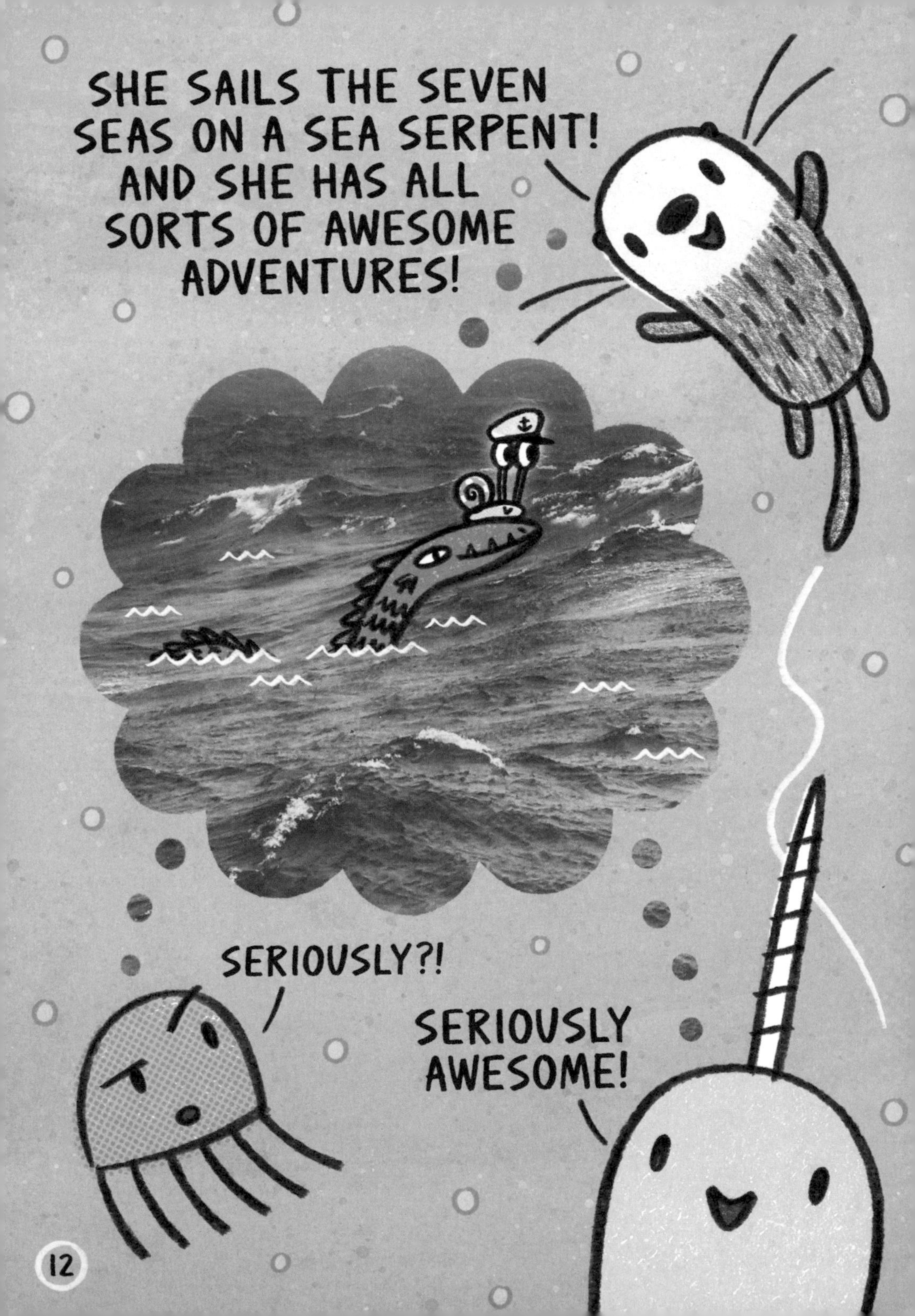
SHE SAILS THE SEVEN SEAS ON A SEA SERPENT! AND SHE HAS ALL SORTS OF AWESOME ADVENTURES!
SERIOUSLY?!
SERIOUSLY AWESOME!

CAPTAIN GOODHART ALSO HAS OODLES OF MARVELOUS MOTTOES!

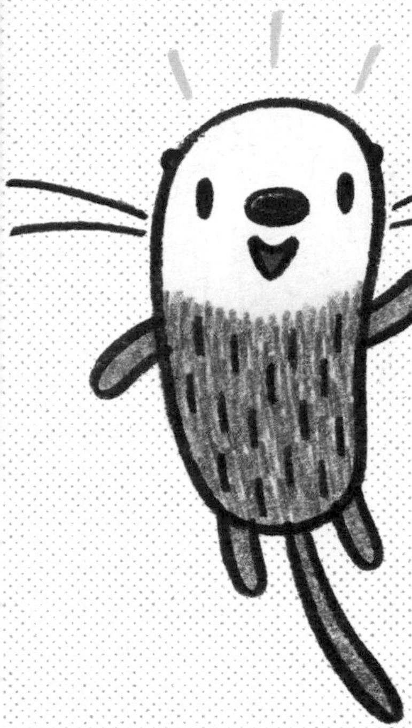

SUCH AS "SEAS THE DAY!"

"GO WITH THE FLOW!"

AND "AHOY, ADVENTURE!"

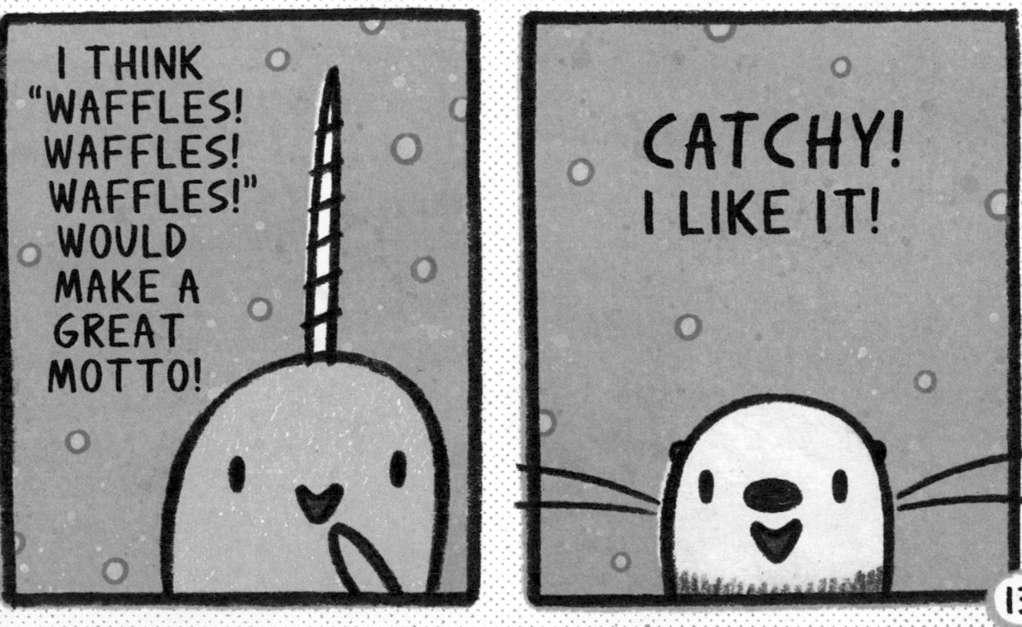
I THINK "WAFFLES! WAFFLES! WAFFLES!" WOULD MAKE A GREAT MOTTO!
CATCHY! I LIKE IT!

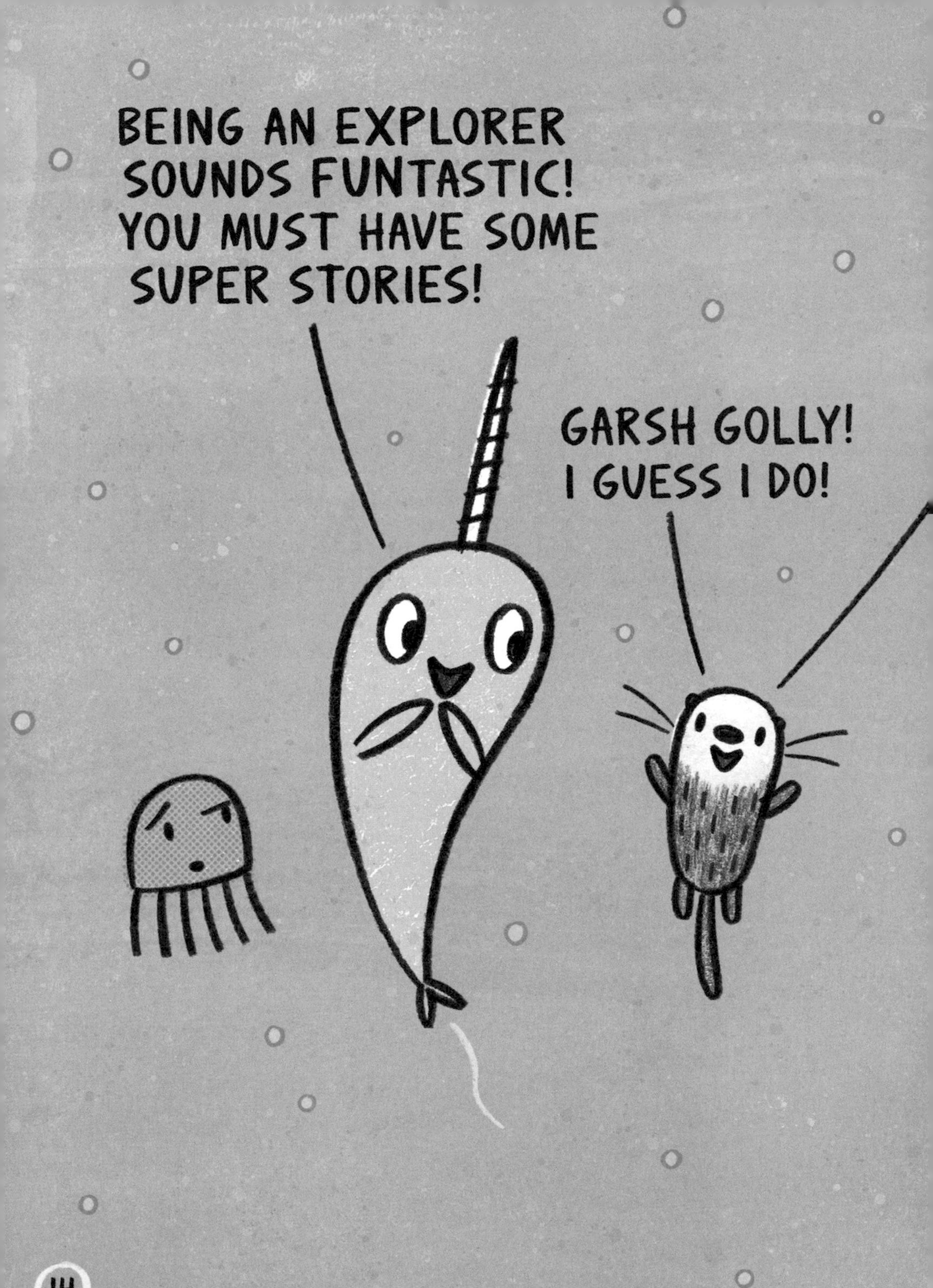
BEING AN EXPLORER SOUNDS FUNTASTIC! YOU MUST HAVE SOME SUPER STORIES!
GARSH GOLLY! I GUESS I DO!

I'VE PARTIED WITH PENGUINS...

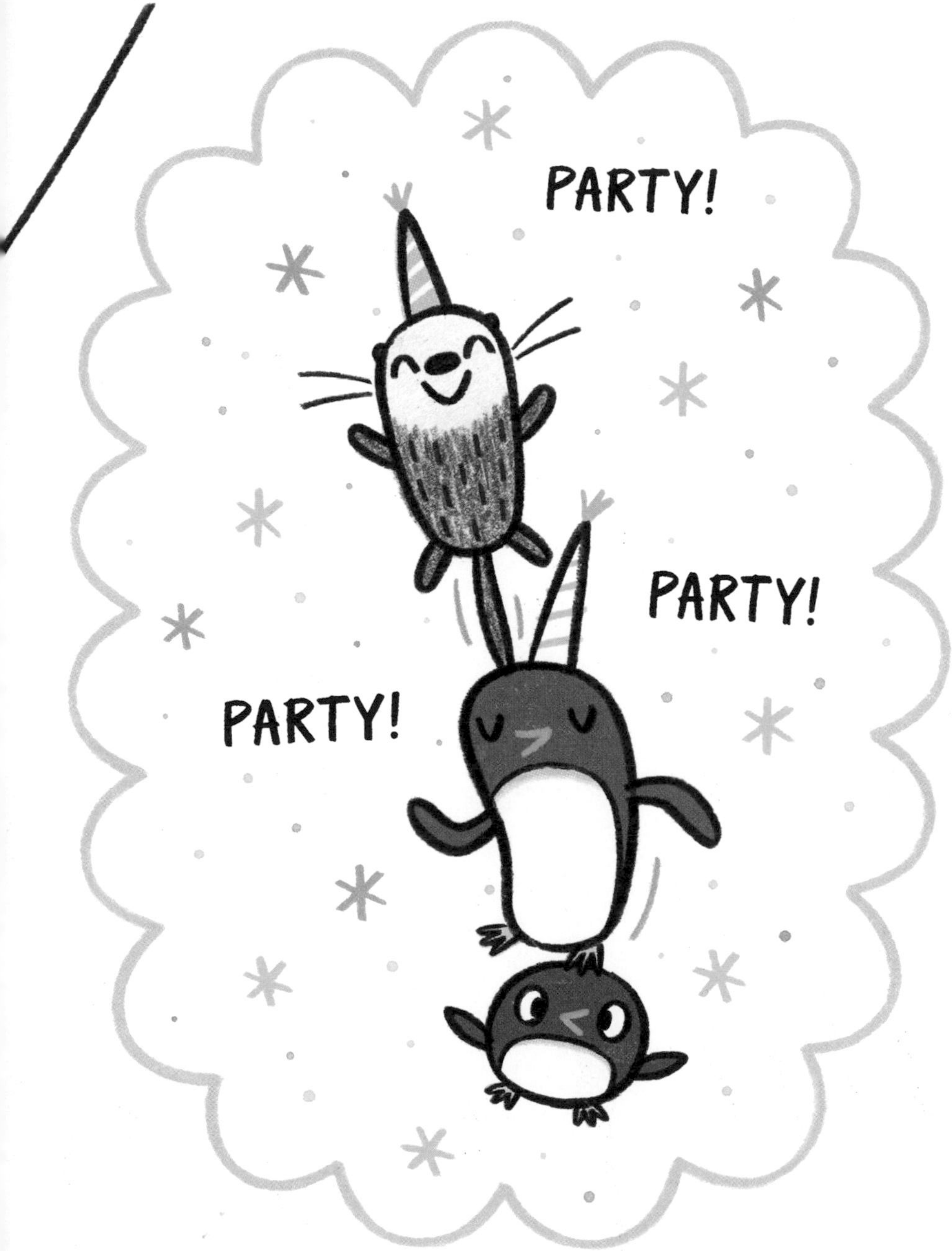
PARTY!
PARTY!
PARTY!

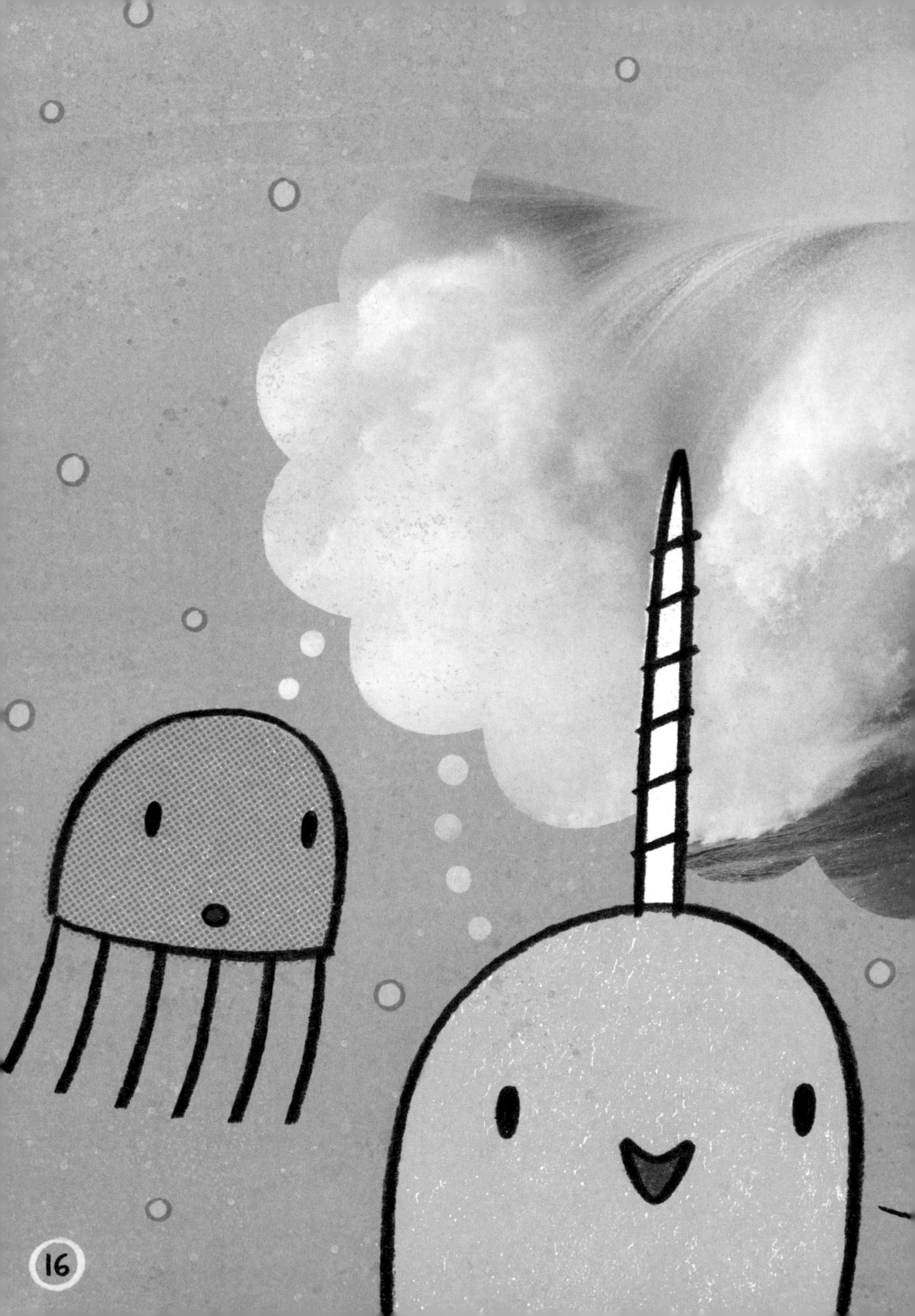

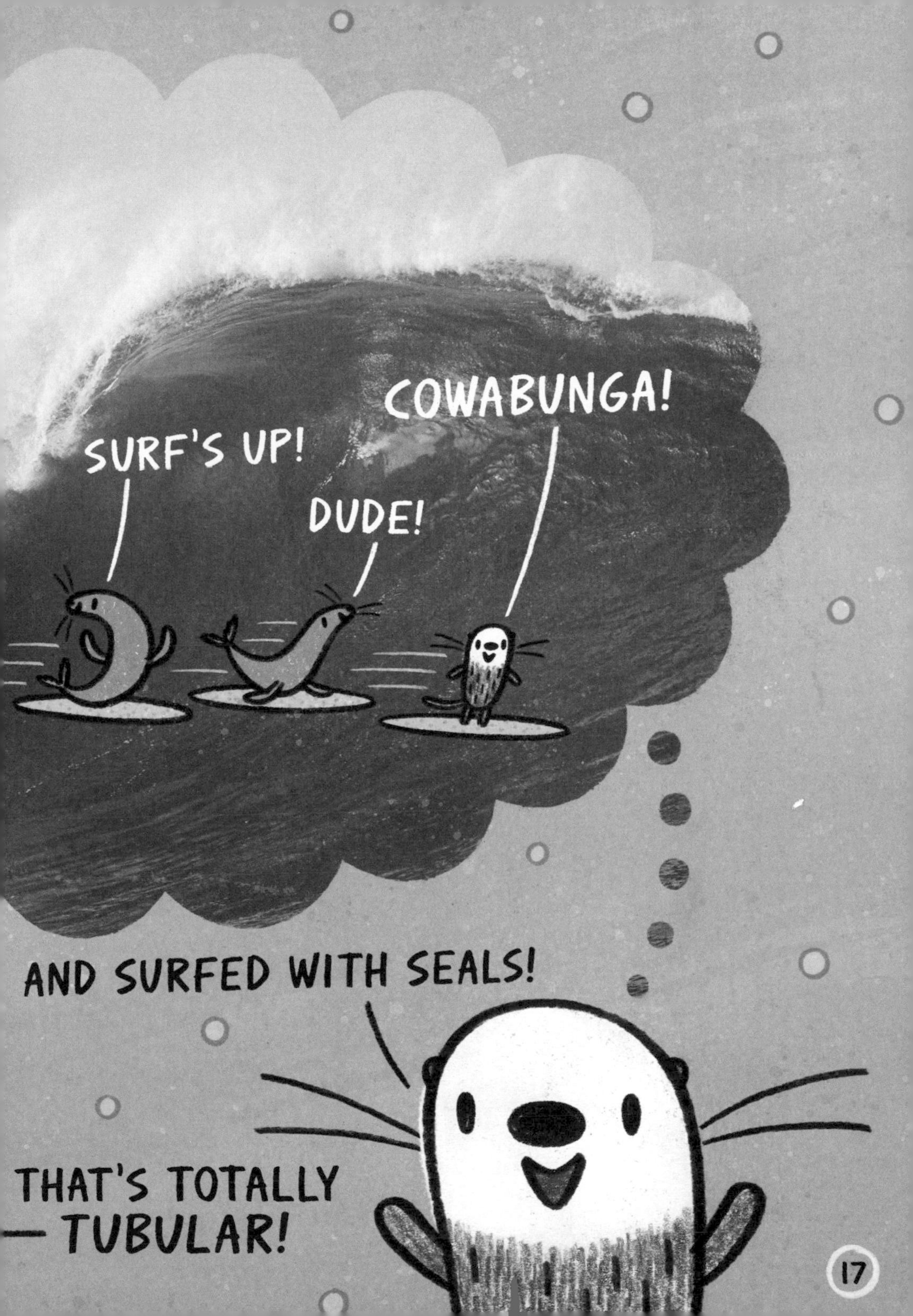
COWABUNGA!
SURF'S UP!
DUDE!
AND SURFED WITH SEALS!
THAT'S TOTALLY
— TUBULAR!

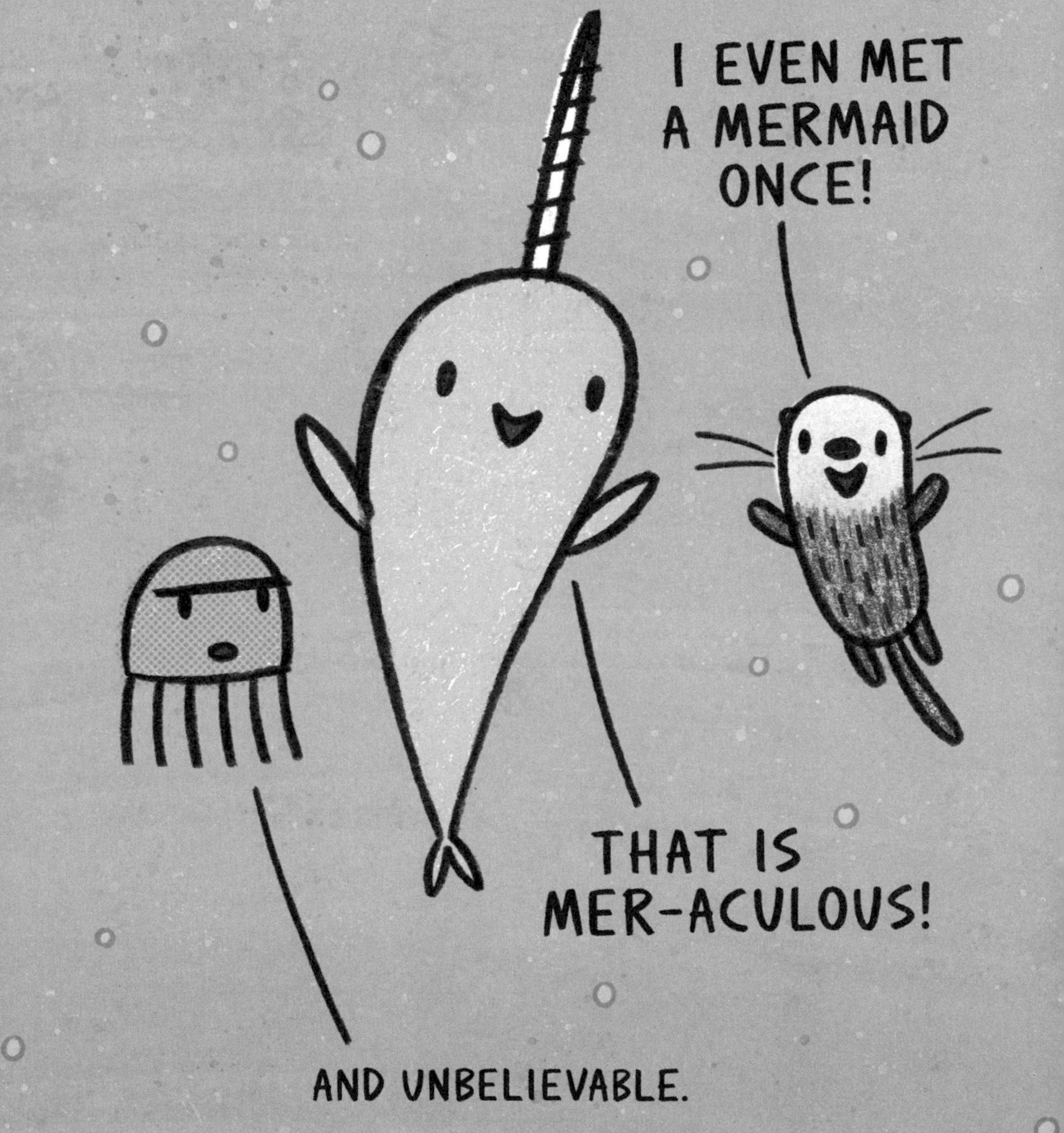
I EVEN MET A MERMAID ONCE!
THAT IS MER-ACULOUS!
AND UNBELIEVABLE.

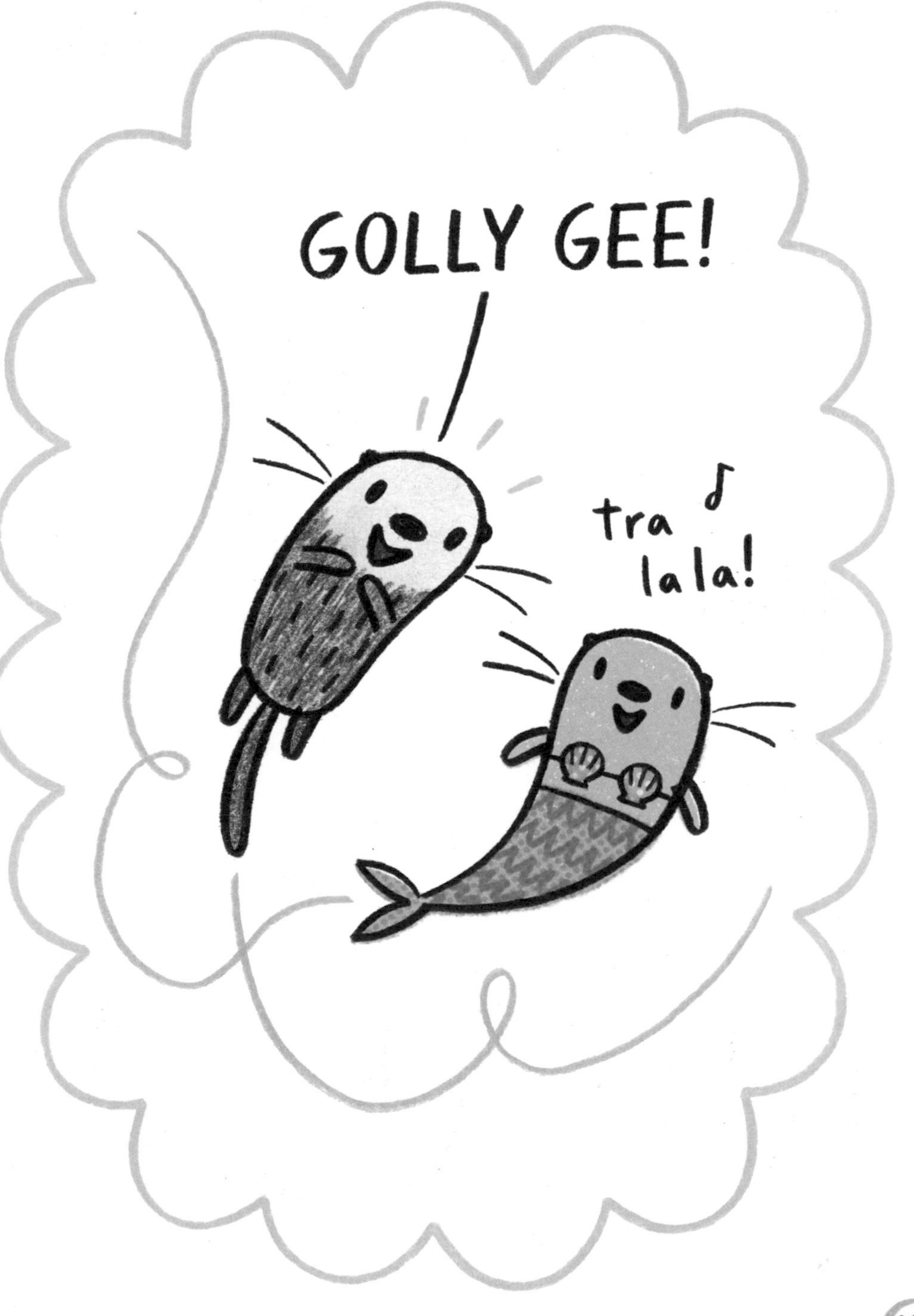
GOLLY GEE!
tra
lala!

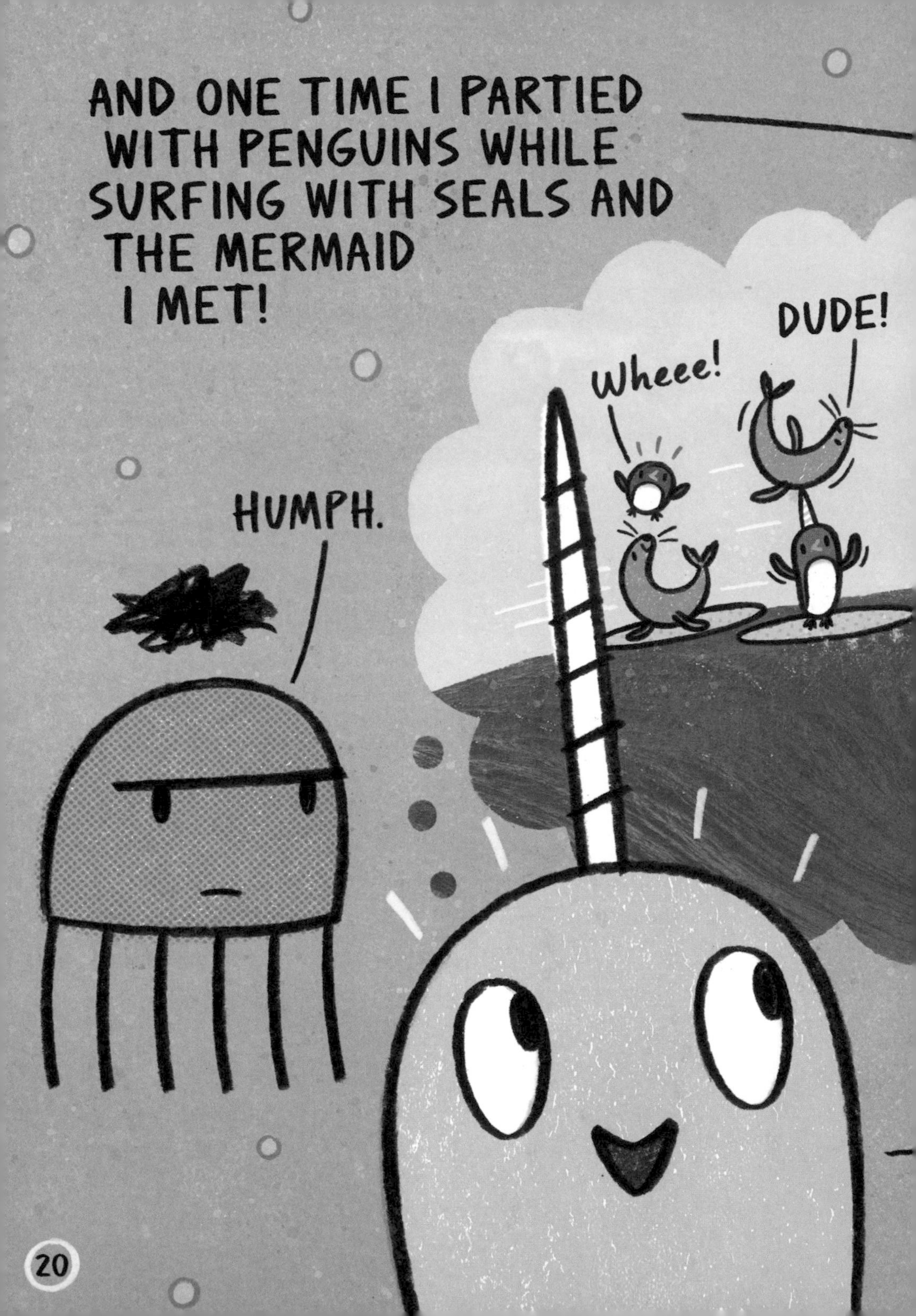
AND ONE TIME I PARTIED WITH PENGUINS WHILE SURFING WITH SEALS AND THE MERMAID I MET!
Wheee!
DUDE!
HUMPH.

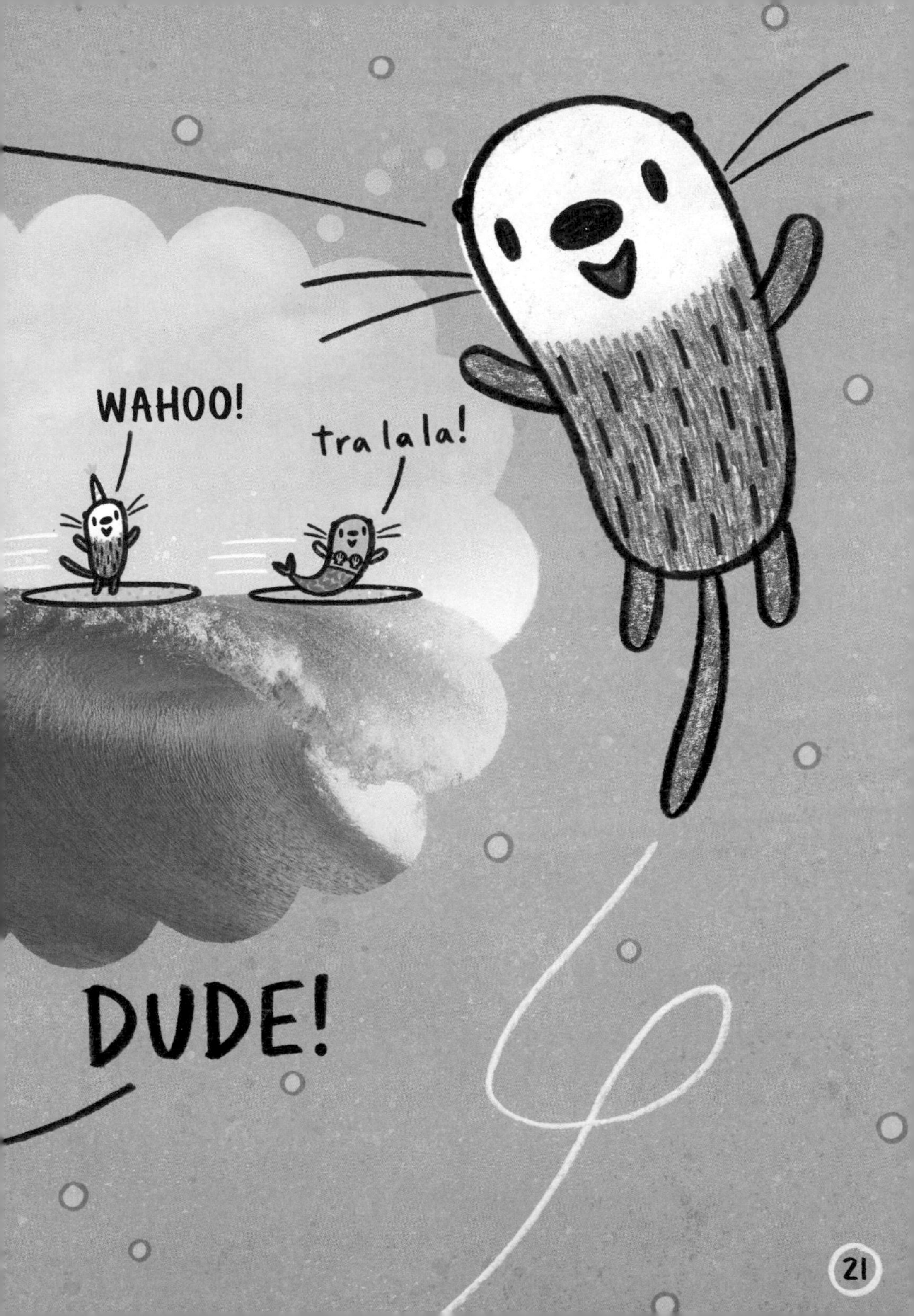
WAHOO!
tra la la!
DUDE!

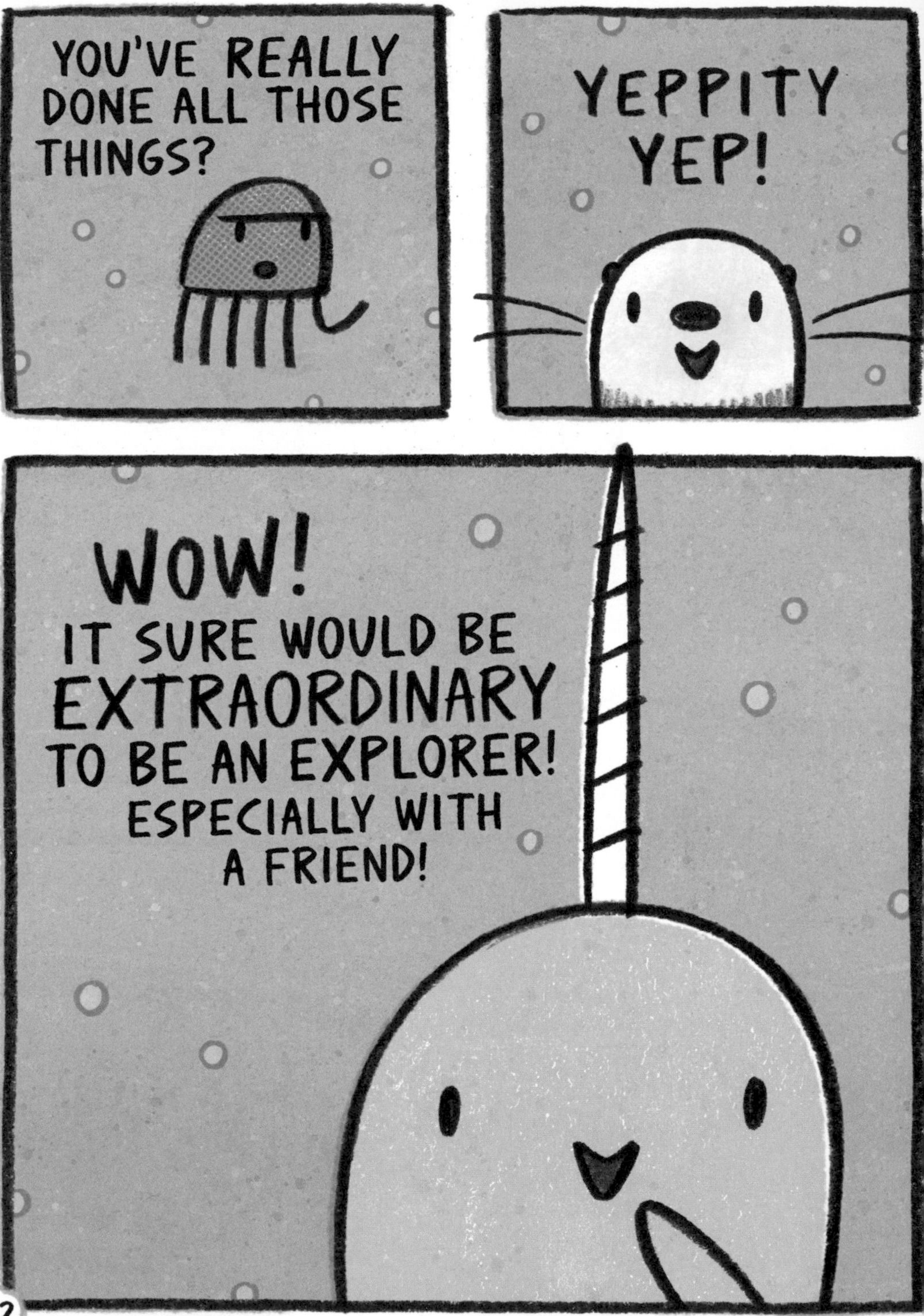
YOU'VE REALLY DONE ALL THOSE THINGS?
YEPPITY YEP!
WOW!
IT SURE WOULD BE EXTRAORDINARY TO BE AN EXPLORER! ESPECIALLY WITH A FRIEND!

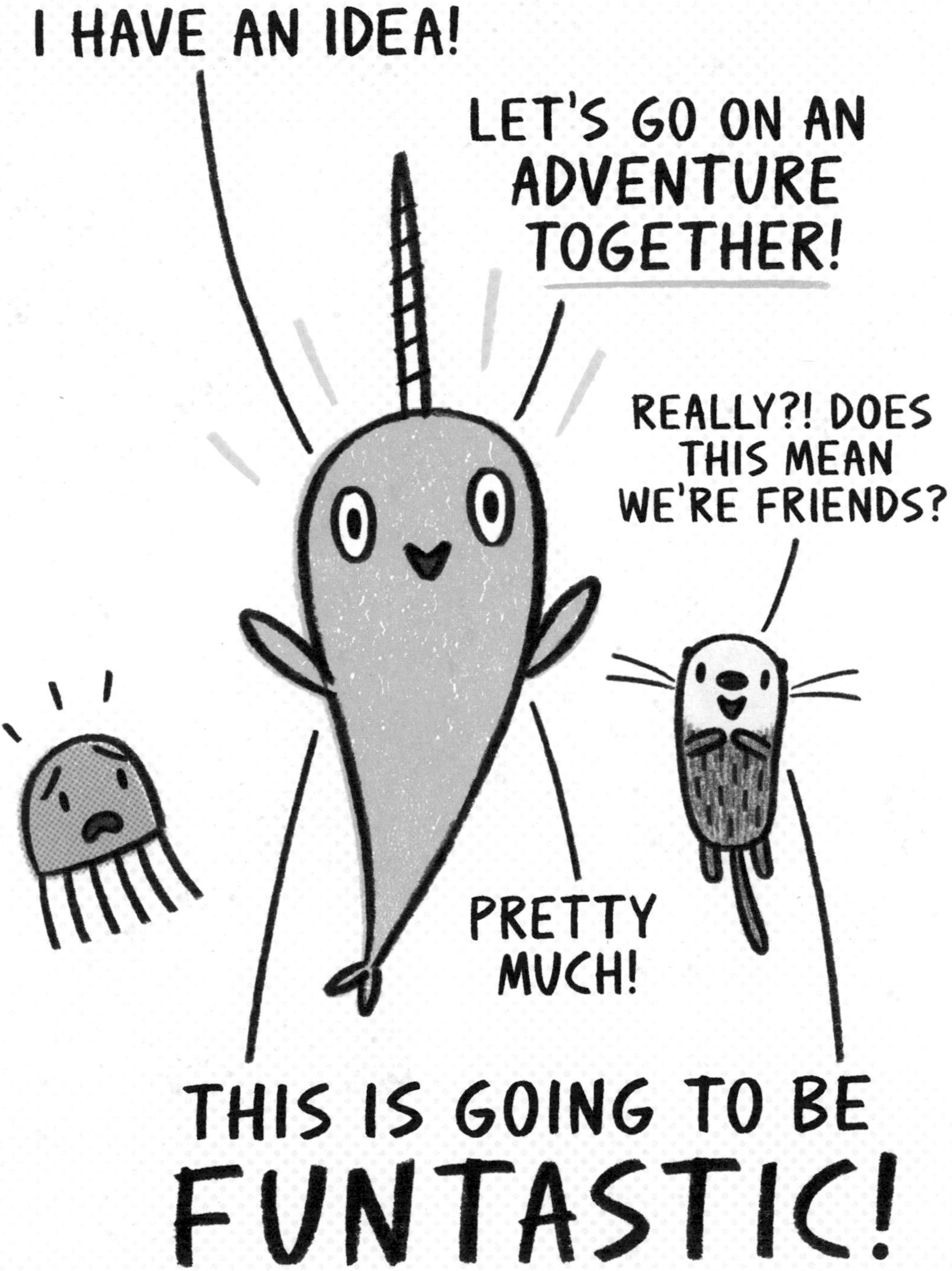
I HAVE AN IDEA!
LET'S GO ON AN ADVENTURE TOGETHER!
REALLY?! DOES THIS MEAN WE'RE FRIENDS?
PRETTY MUCH!
THIS IS GOING TO BE FUNTASTIC!

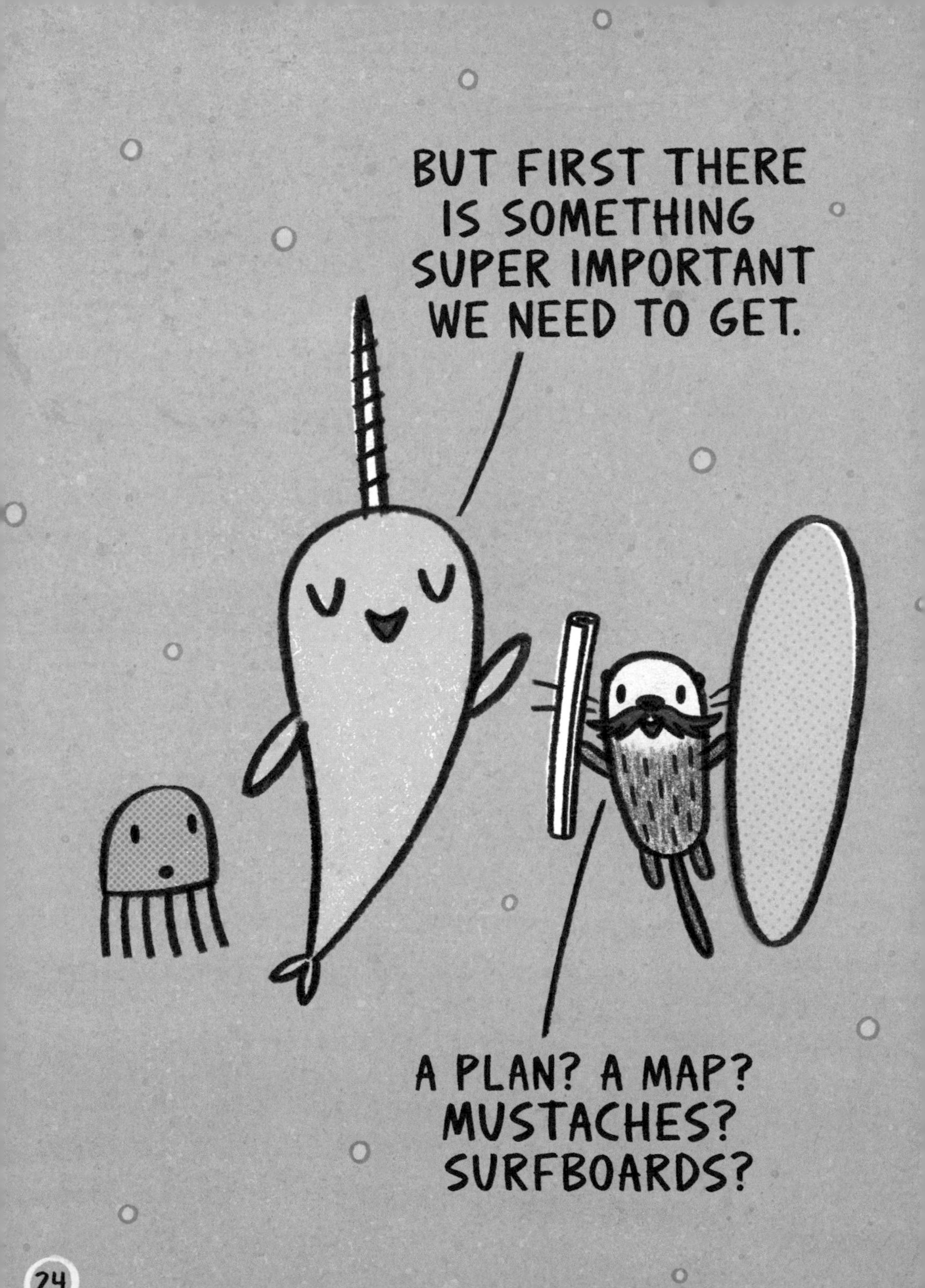
BUT FIRST THERE IS SOMETHING SUPER IMPORTANT WE NEED TO GET.
A PLAN? A MAP? MUSTACHES? SURFBOARDS?

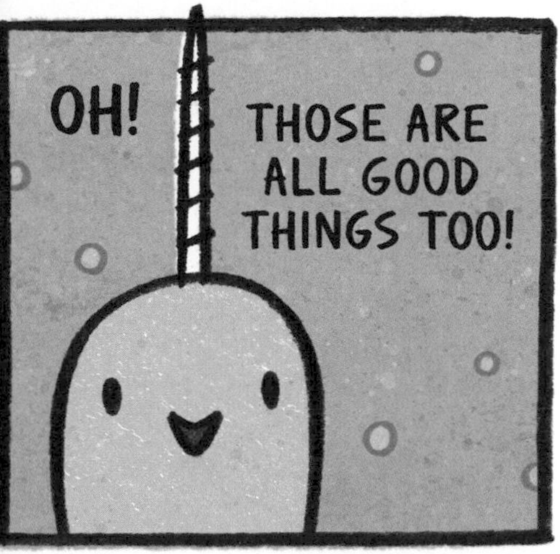
OH!
THOSE ARE ALL GOOD THINGS TOO!

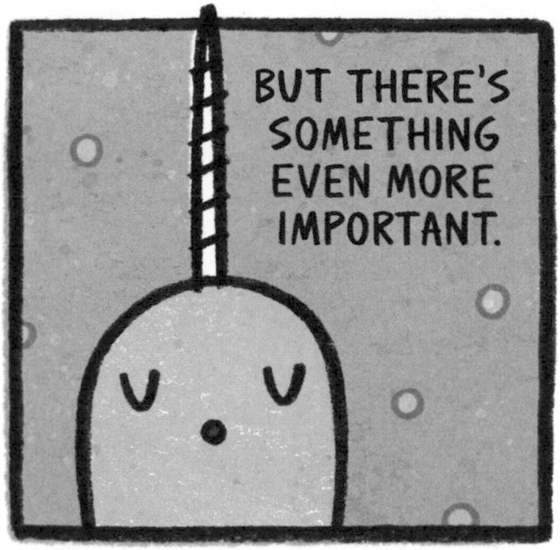
BUT THERE'S SOMETHING EVEN MORE IMPORTANT.

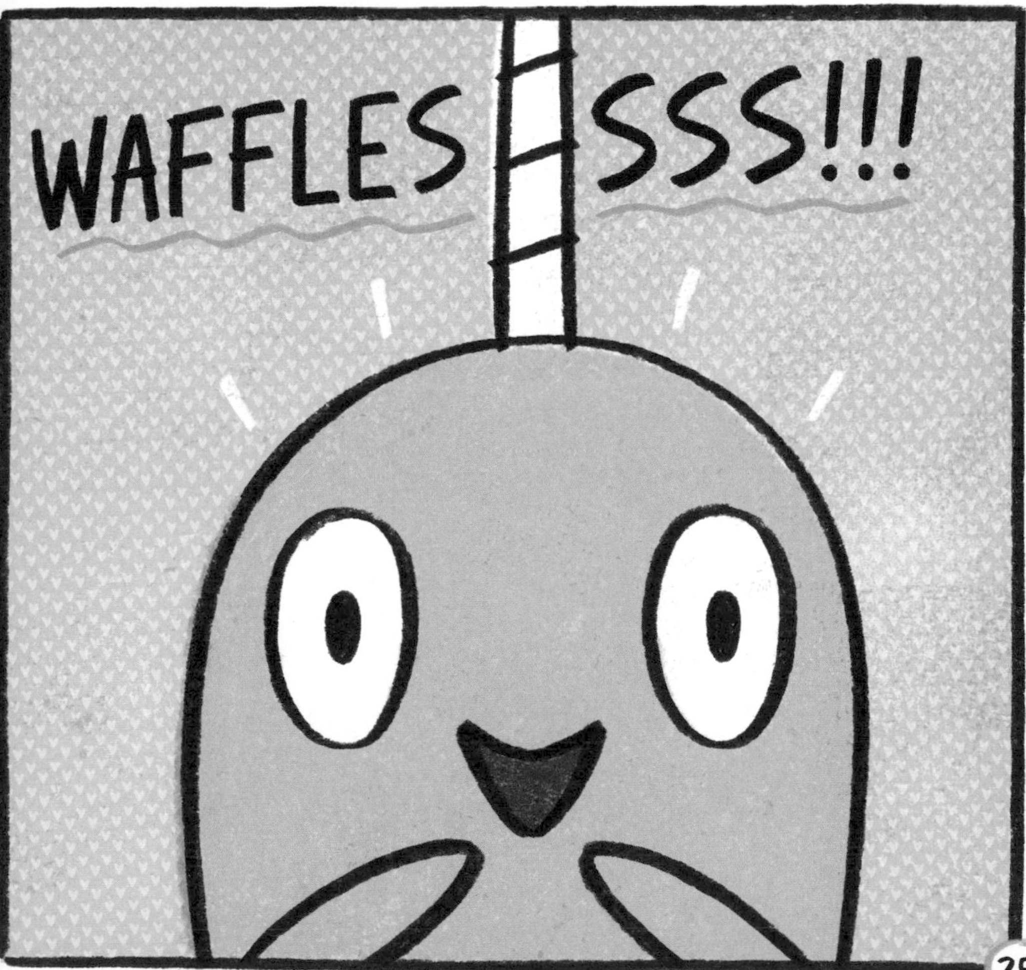
WAFFLESSSS!!!

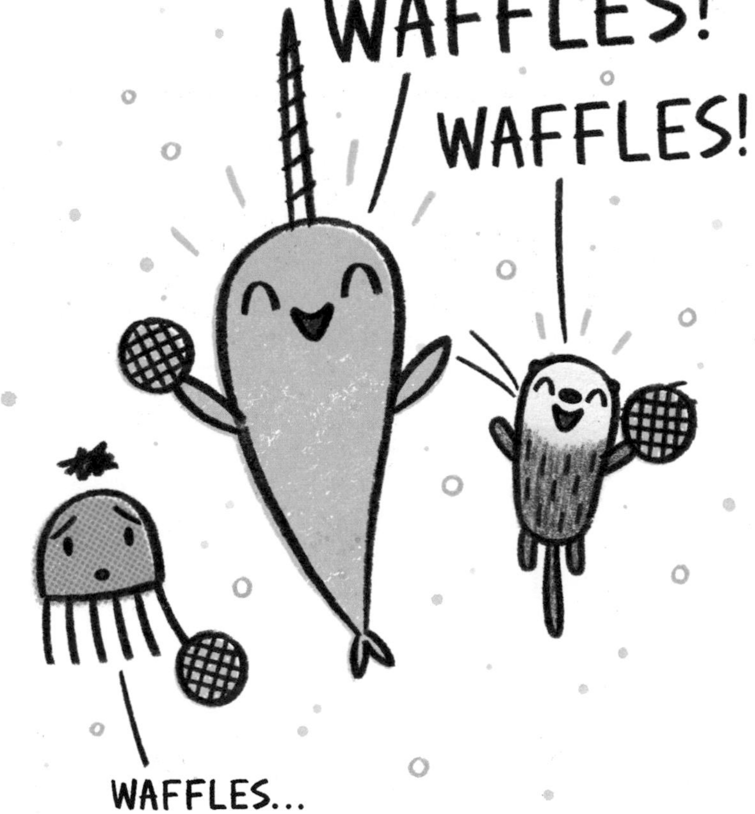
WAFFLES!
WAFFLES!
WAFFLES...

OTTERLY AWW-SOME FACTS

REAL FACTS ABOUT A REALLY ADORABLE CREATURE

THERE ARE 13 KINDS (SPECIES) OF OTTER IN THE WORLD.*

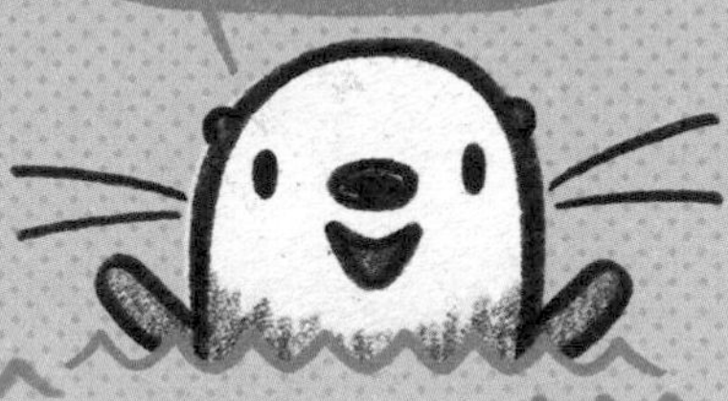
WE'RE ALL KINDS OF AWESOME!

OTTERS LIVE ON EVERY CONTINENT EXCEPT FOR AUSTRALIA AND ANTARCTICA. THEY ARE USUALLY FOUND IN OR NEAR WATER.

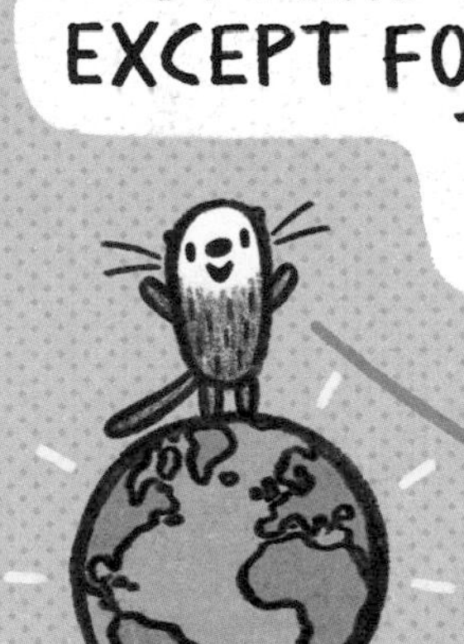
WHAT A WATERFUL WORLD!

* 12 OF THE 13 SPECIES ARE LISTED AS THREATENED, VULNERABLE OR ENDANGERED.

OTTER FACTS

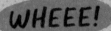
WHEEE!

OTTERS CAN BE VERY PLAYFUL AND ARE KNOWN TO ENJOY SLIDES.

WHEN IN THE WATER A GROUP OF SEA OTTERS IS CALLED A RAFT. SOMETIMES RAFTING SEA OTTERS HOLD PAWS TO STAY TOGETHER WHEN SLEEPING.

MY PRECIOUS!

SEA OTTERS EACH HAVE A "FAVORITE" ROCK THEY KEEP IN A FOLD OF SKIN UNDER A FORELEG. THEY USE THE ROCK TO SMASH OPEN CLAMS AND SHELLFISH TO EAT.

FUR-THER FACTS

BUBBLES!

SEA OTTERS USE BUBBLES TO STAY WARM! THEY TRAP BUBBLES IN THEIR FUR CREATING A "BLANKET" OF AIR THAT HELPS TO INSULATE THEM.

FUR SURE!

CALIFORNIA SEA OTTERS HAVE THE DENSEST FUR OF ANY MAMMAL ON THE PLANET: UP TO ABOUT A MILLION HAIRS PER 6.5 CM^2 (~1 IN.^{2}).

SOME ~~OTTER~~ FACTS
JELLYFISH

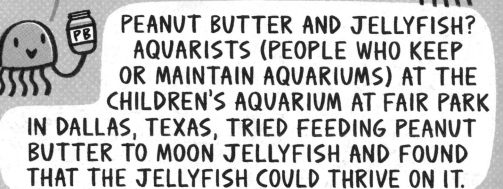

NOT BAD!

PEANUT BUTTER AND JELLYFISH? AQUARISTS (PEOPLE WHO KEEP OR MAINTAIN AQUARIUMS) AT THE CHILDREN'S AQUARIUM AT FAIR PARK IN DALLAS, TEXAS, TRIED FEEDING PEANUT BUTTER TO MOON JELLYFISH AND FOUND THAT THE JELLYFISH COULD THRIVE ON IT.

A JELLYFISH'S BODY IS MADE UP OF ABOUT 95% WATER!

WHAT-ER?!

SOME JELLYFISH CAN GLOW IN THE DARK!

JEALOUS JELLY

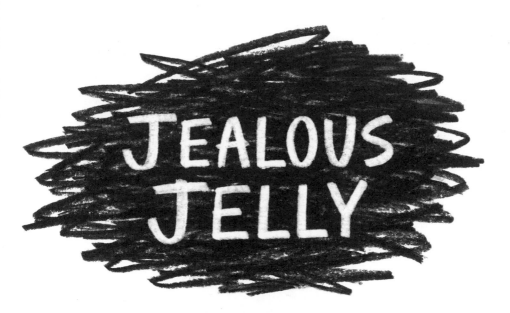

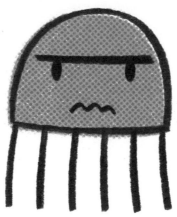

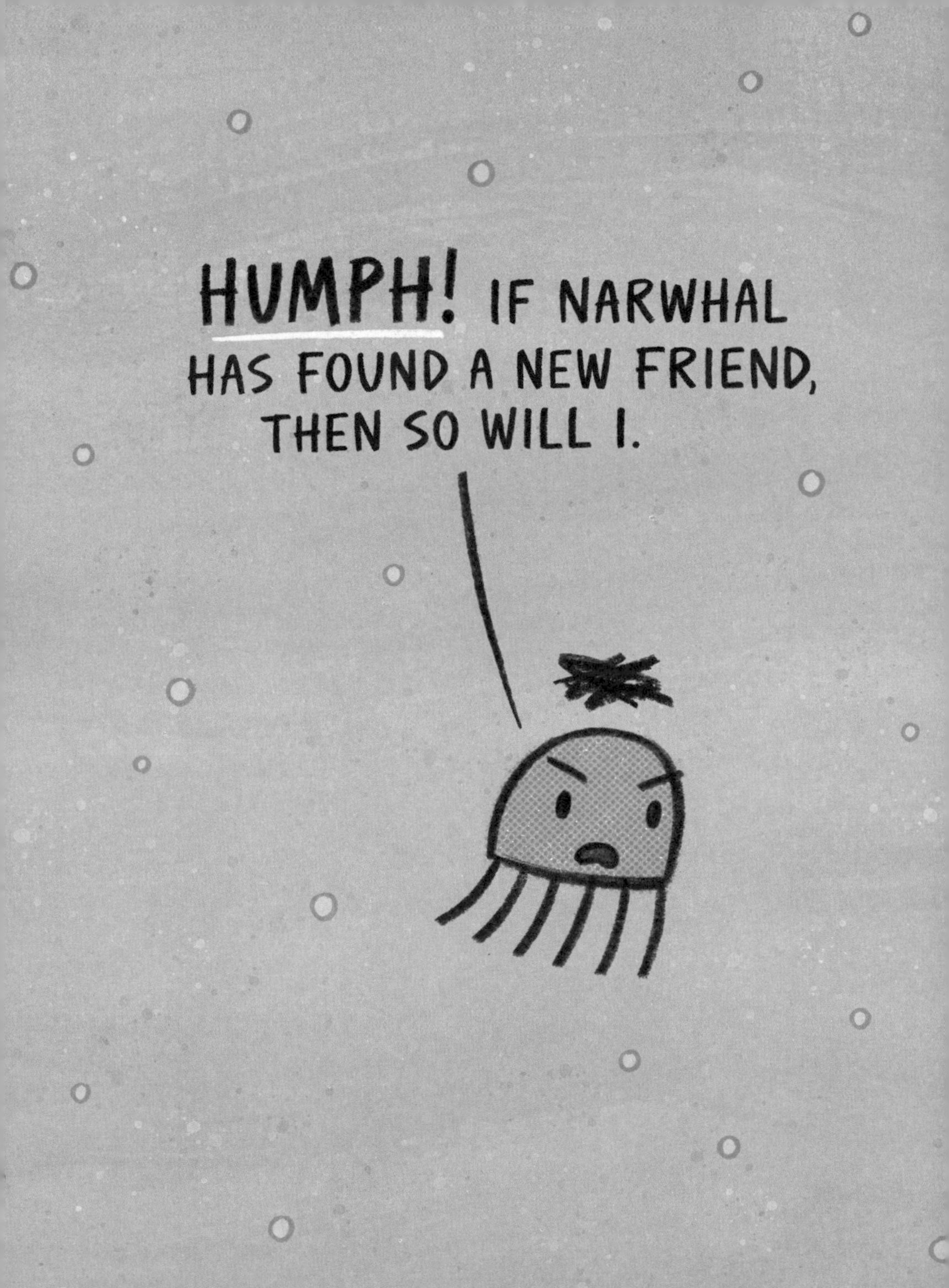
HUMPH! IF NARWHAL HAS FOUND A NEW FRIEND, THEN SO WILL I.

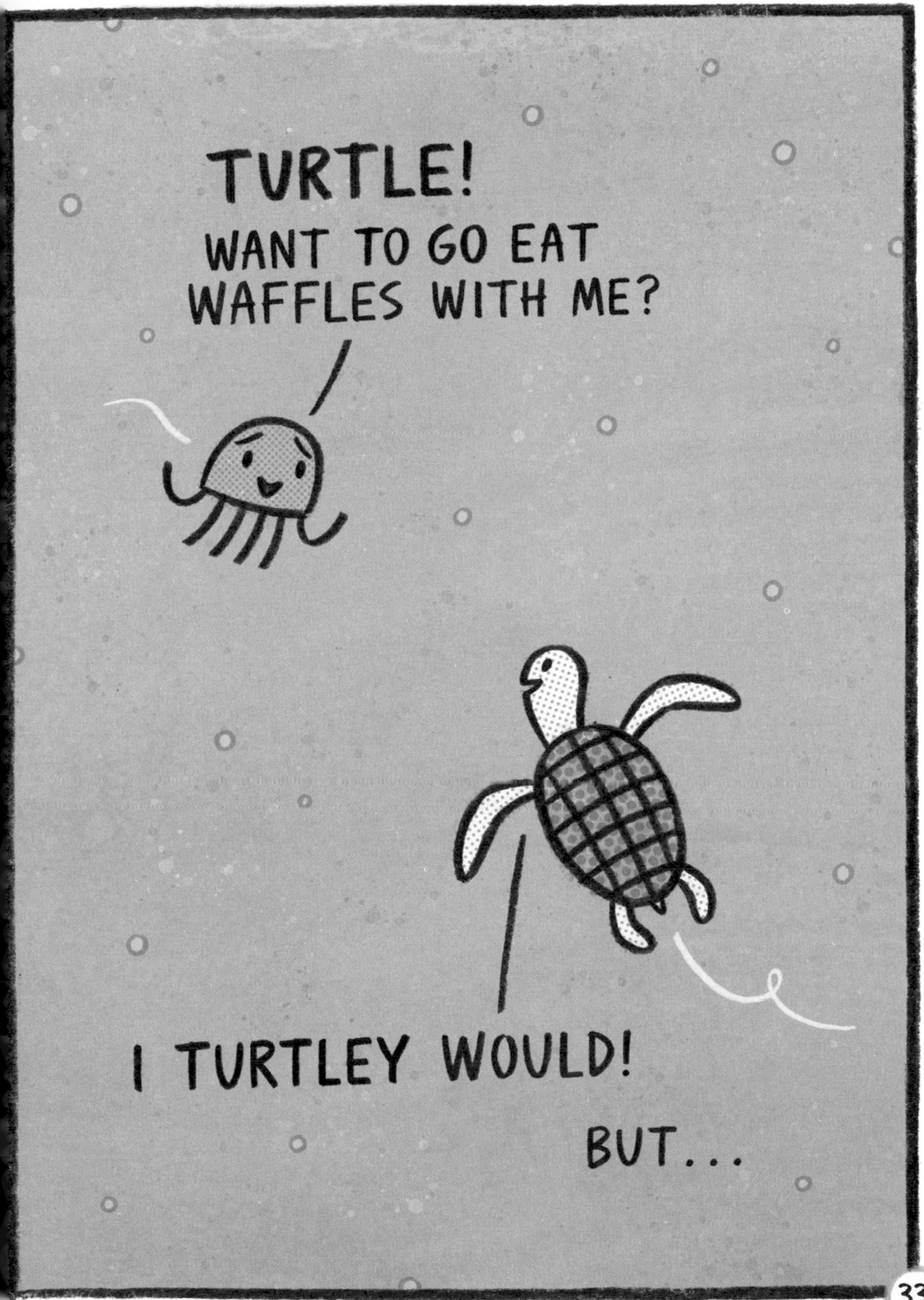
TURTLE!
WANT TO GO EAT WAFFLES WITH ME?
I TURTLEY WOULD!
BUT...

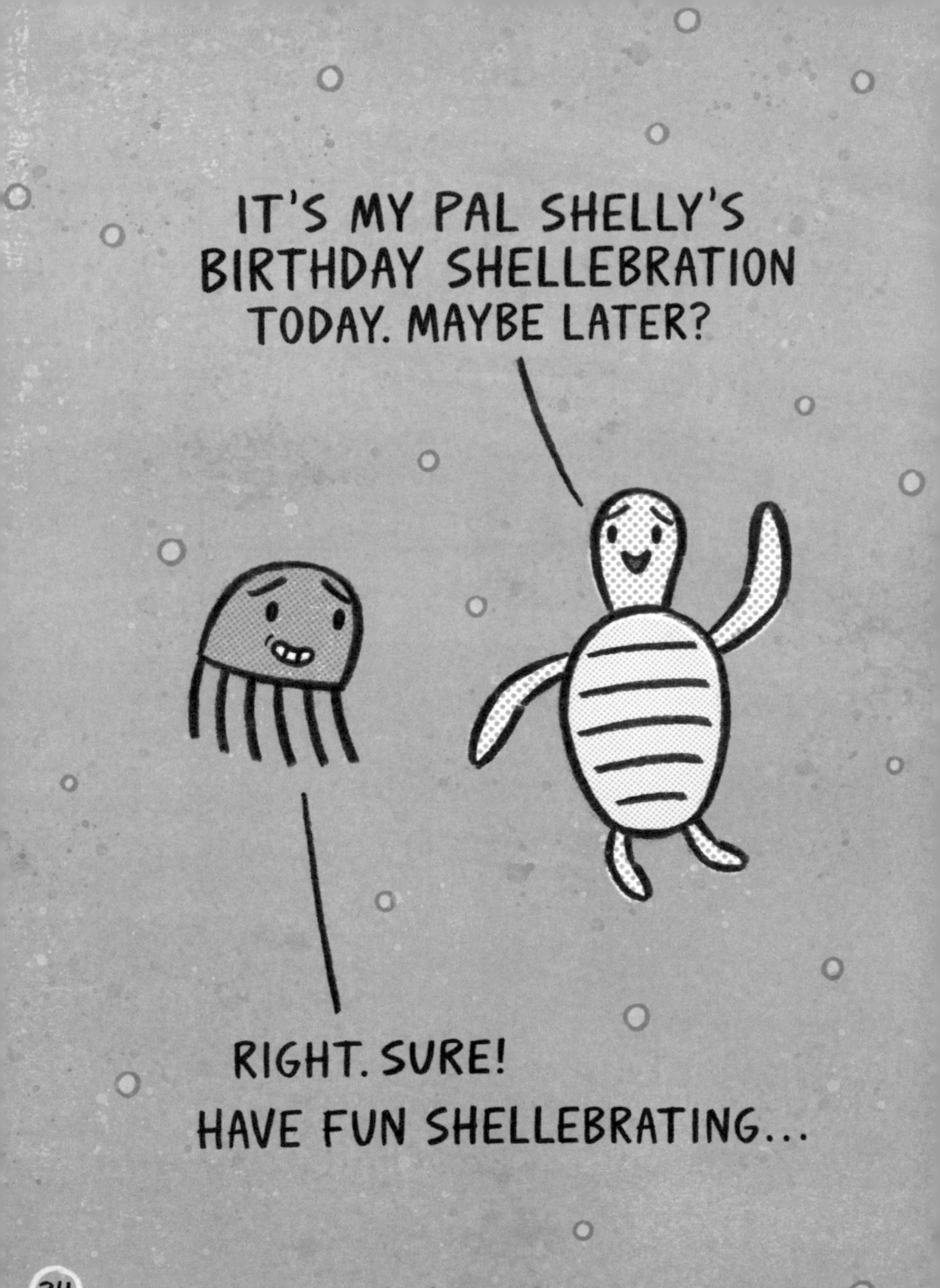
IT'S MY PAL SHELLY'S BIRTHDAY SHELLEBRATION TODAY. MAYBE LATER?
RIGHT. SURE!
HAVE FUN SHELLEBRATING...

SHARK!
WHAT'S UP?

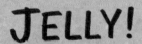

JELLY!
I'M OFF TO PLAY BUOY BALL
WITH MY BEST BUD, OCTOPUS!

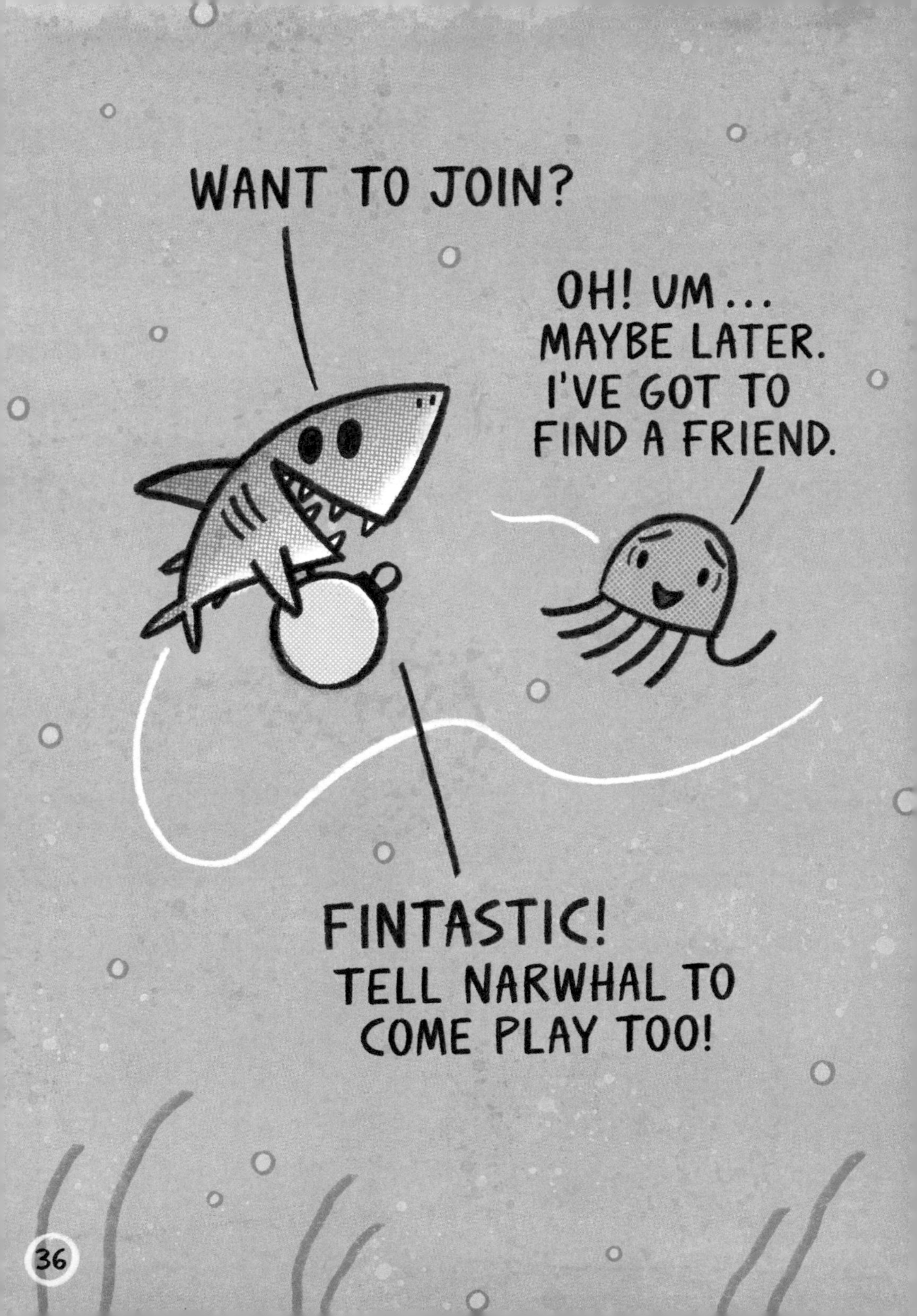
WANT TO JOIN?
OH! UM... MAYBE LATER. I'VE GOT TO FIND A FRIEND.
FINTASTIC! TELL NARWHAL TO COME PLAY TOO!

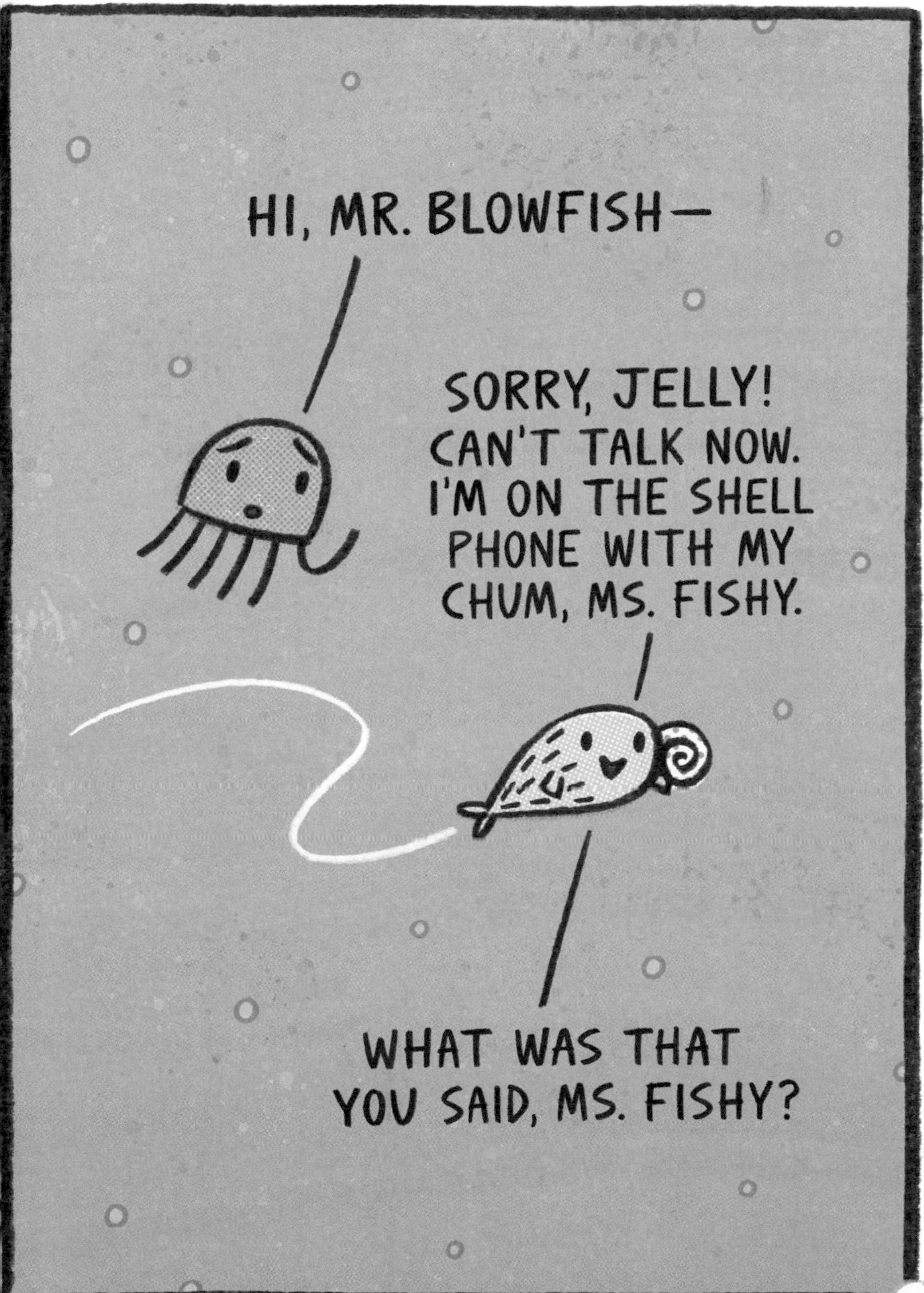
HI, MR. BLOWFISH—
SORRY, JELLY! CAN'T TALK NOW. I'M ON THE SHELL PHONE WITH MY CHUM, MS. FISHY.
WHAT WAS THAT YOU SAID, MS. FISHY?

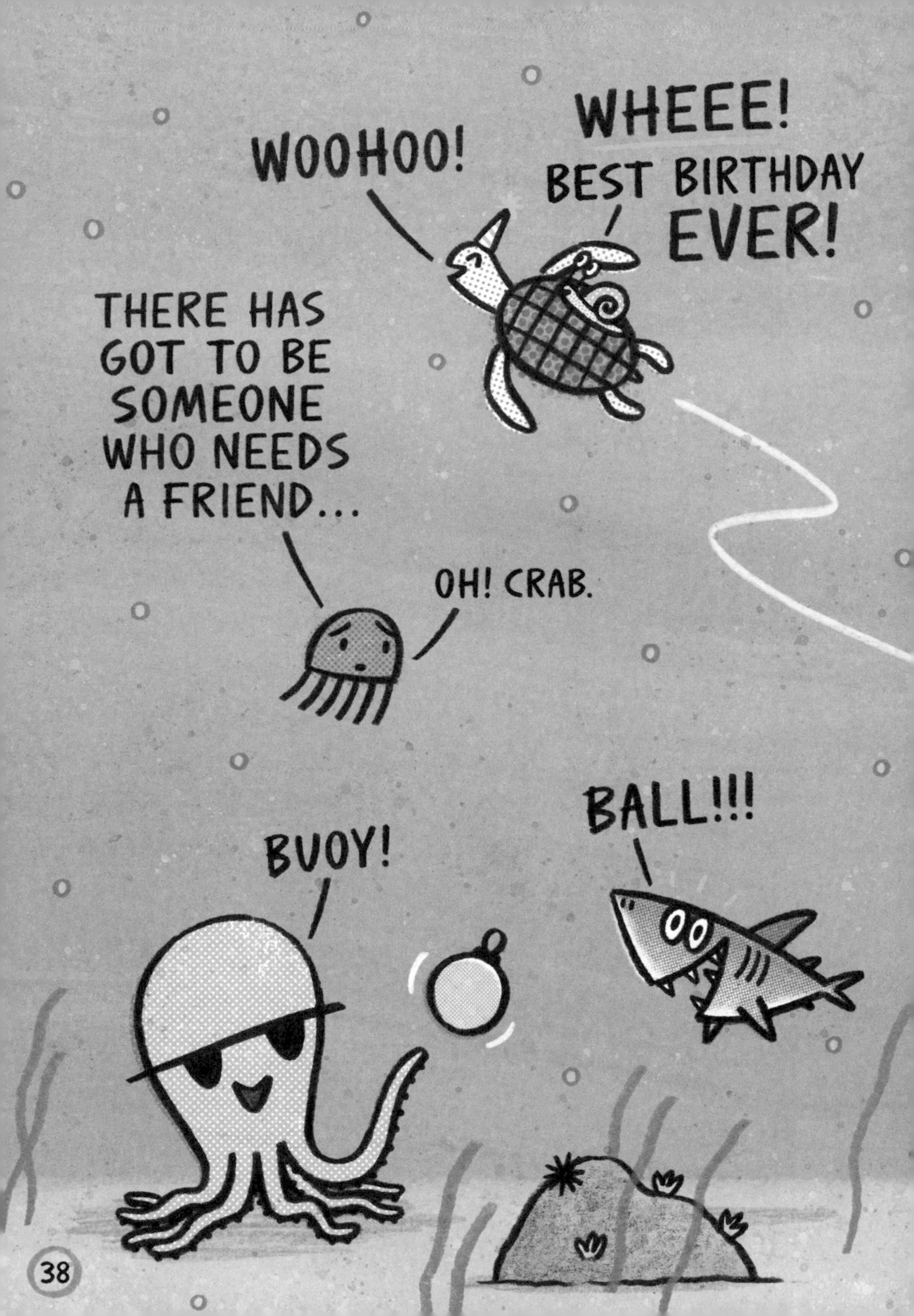
WHEEE!
WOOHOO!
BEST BIRTHDAY EVER!
THERE HAS GOT TO BE SOMEONE WHO NEEDS A FRIEND...
OH! CRAB.
BALL!!!
BUOY!

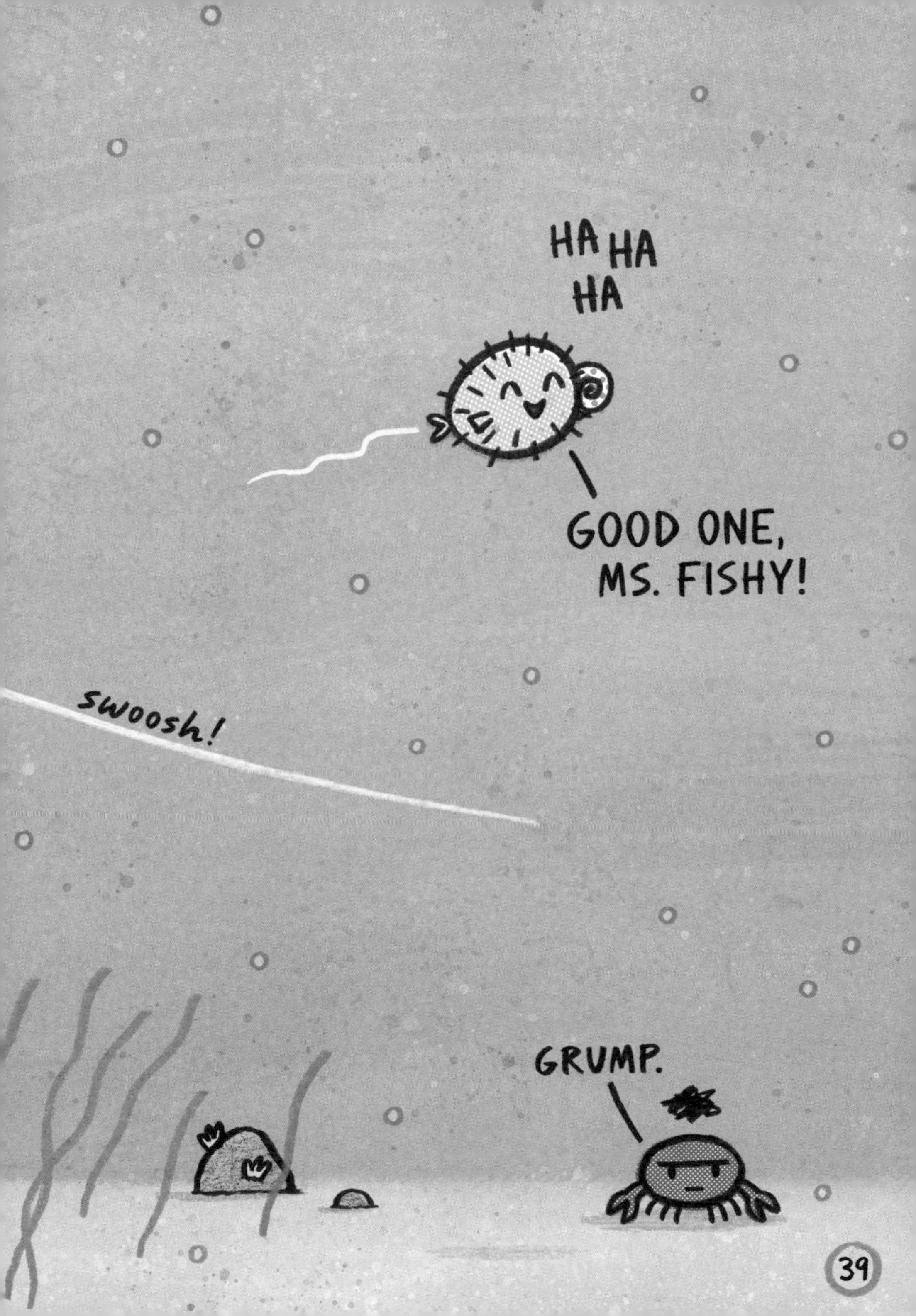
HA HA HA
GOOD ONE, MS. FISHY!
swoosh!
GRUMP.

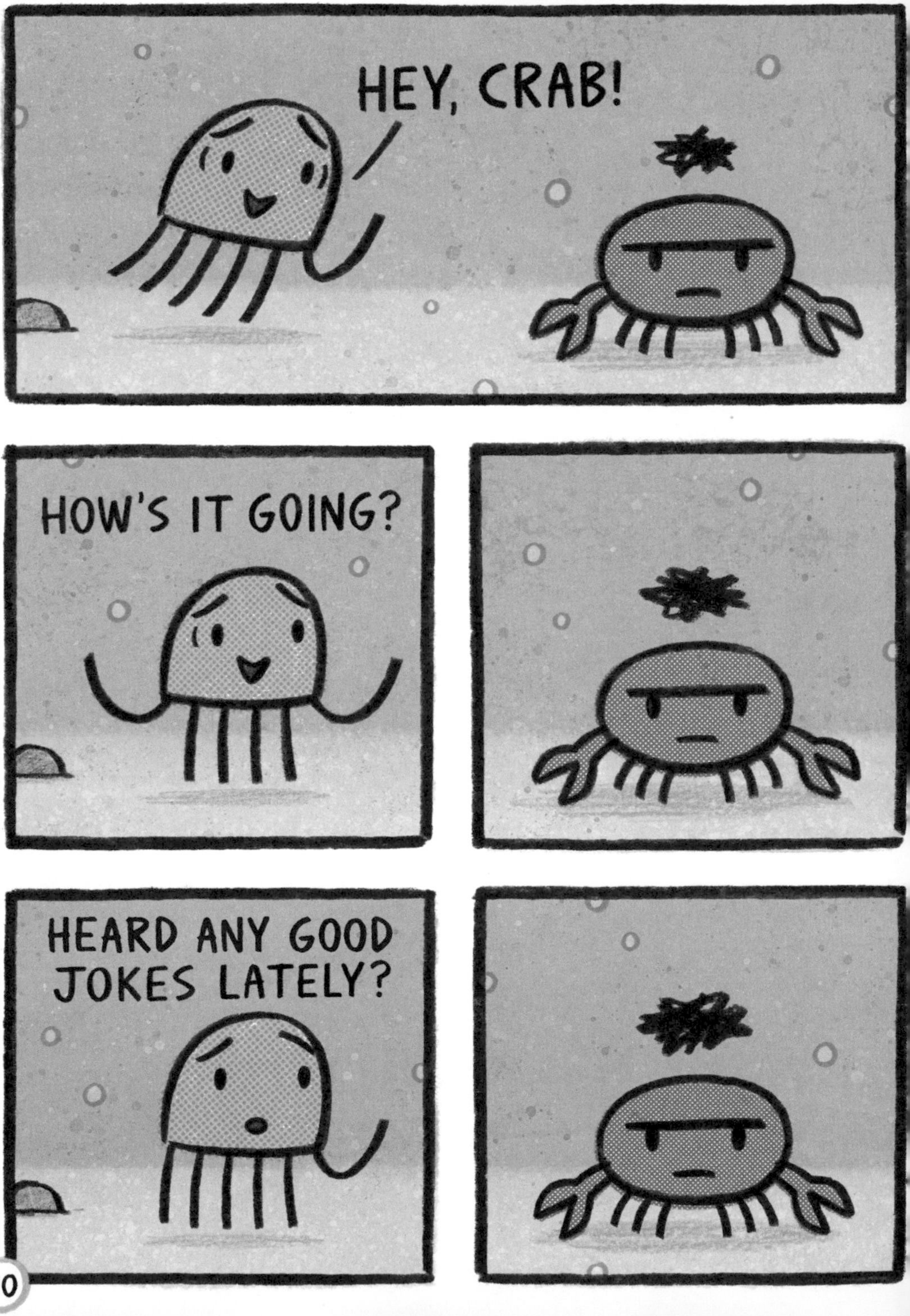
HEY, CRAB!
HOW'S IT GOING?
HEARD ANY GOOD JOKES LATELY?

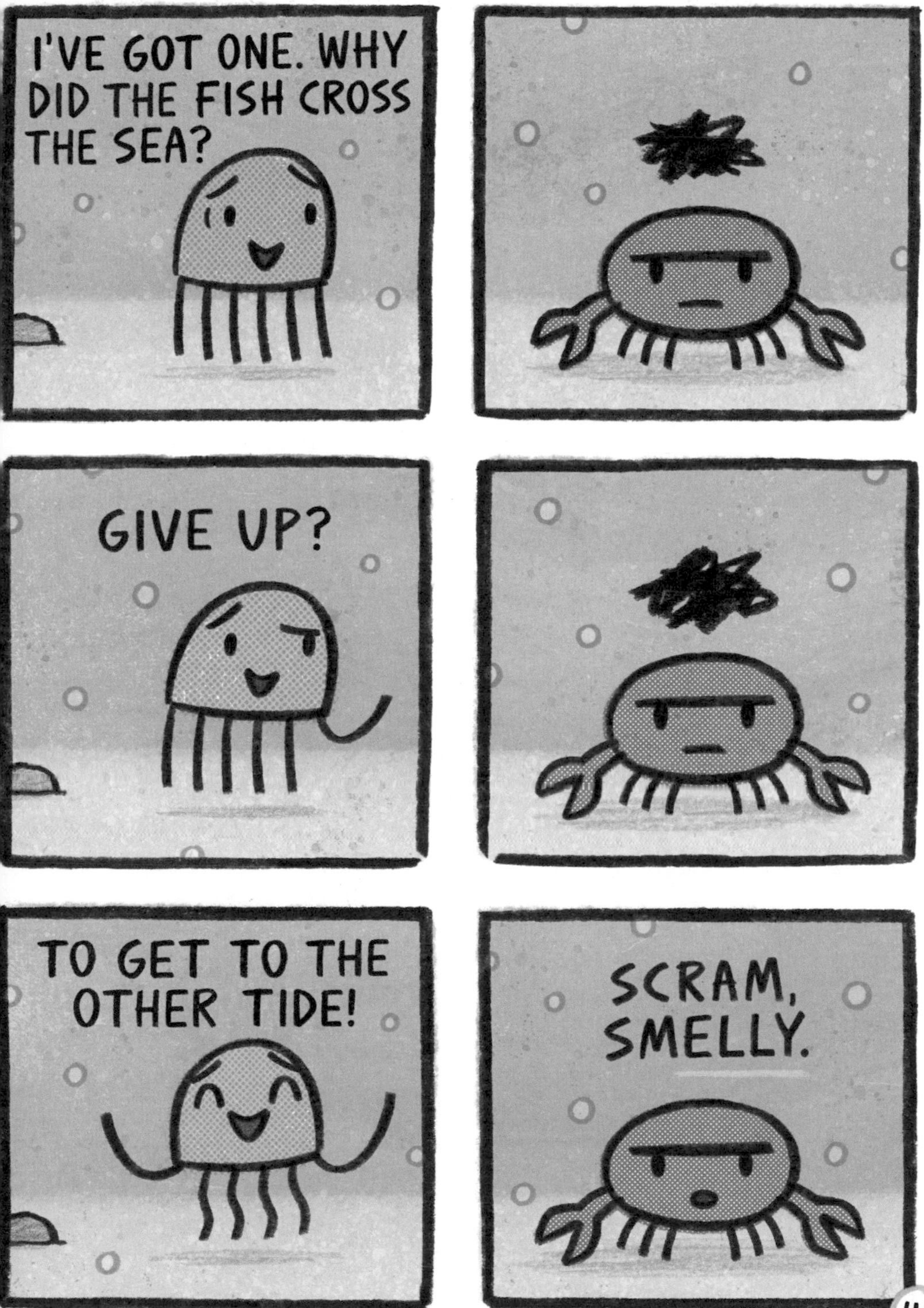
I'VE GOT ONE. WHY DID THE FISH CROSS THE SEA?
GIVE UP?
TO GET TO THE OTHER TIDE!
SCRAM, SMELLY.

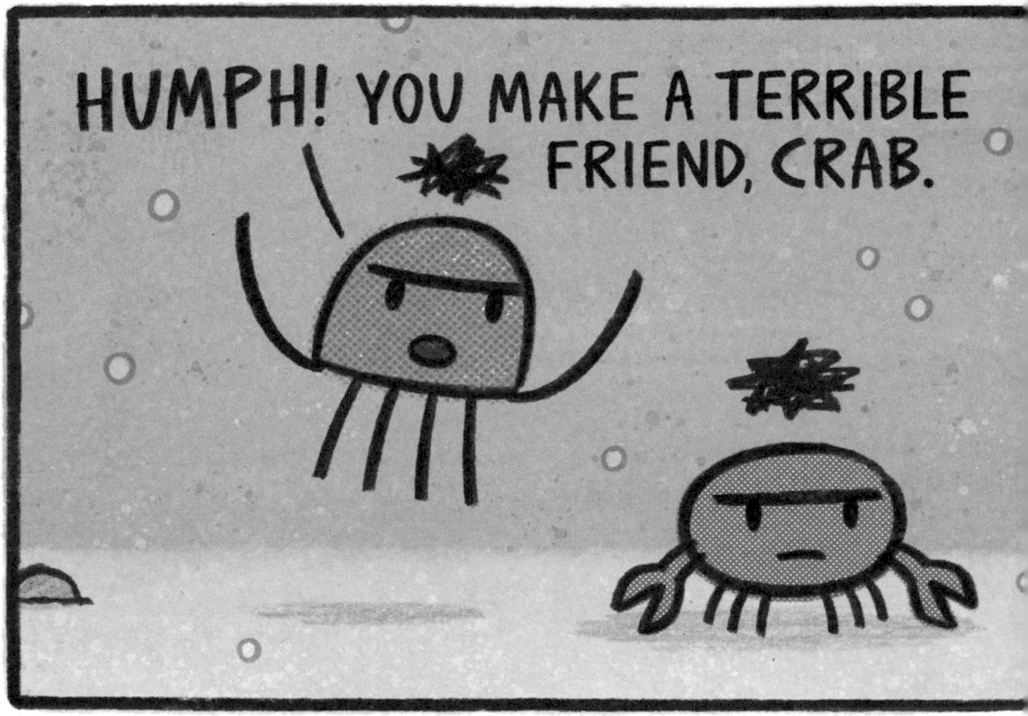
HUMPH! YOU MAKE A TERRIBLE FRIEND, CRAB.

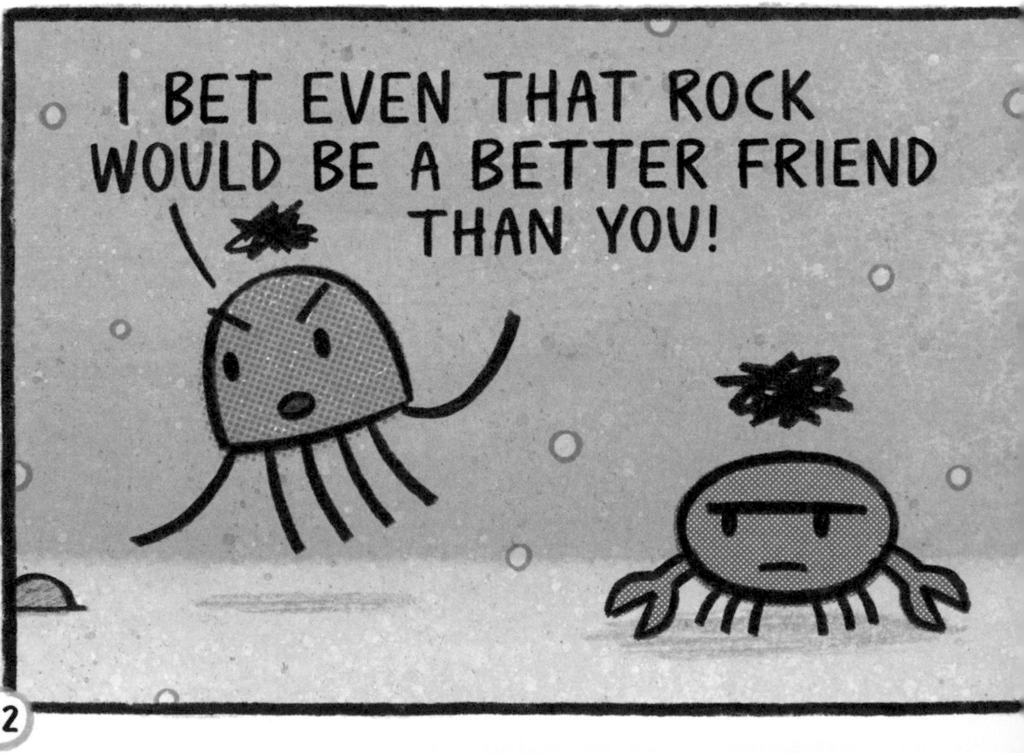
I BET EVEN THAT ROCK WOULD BE A BETTER FRIEND THAN YOU!

THAT'S IT!

ROCKY, I THINK
YOU'RE GOING
TO BE ONE ROCK-
SOLID FRIEND.

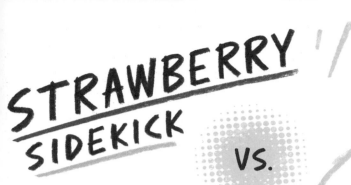

STRAWBERRY SIDEKICK VS. THE dEVILed EGG

by Jelly and Rocky

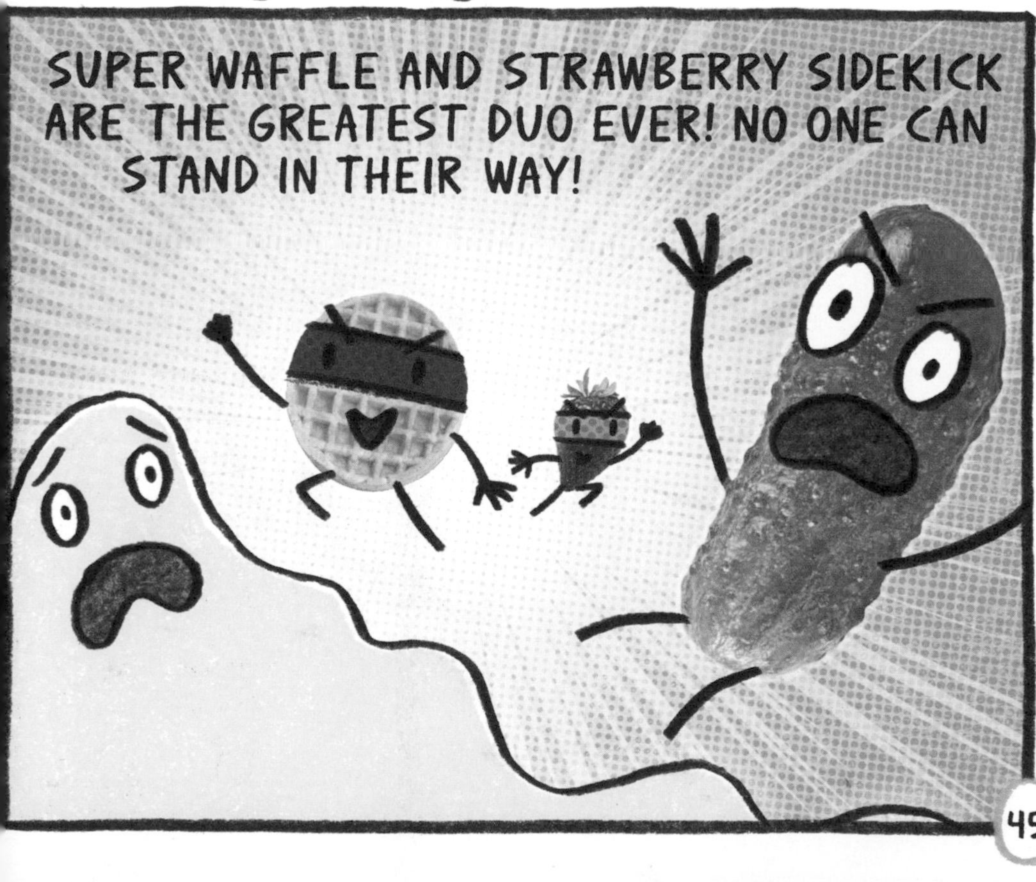
SUPER WAFFLE AND STRAWBERRY SIDEKICK ARE THE GREATEST DUO EVER! NO ONE CAN STAND IN THEIR WAY!

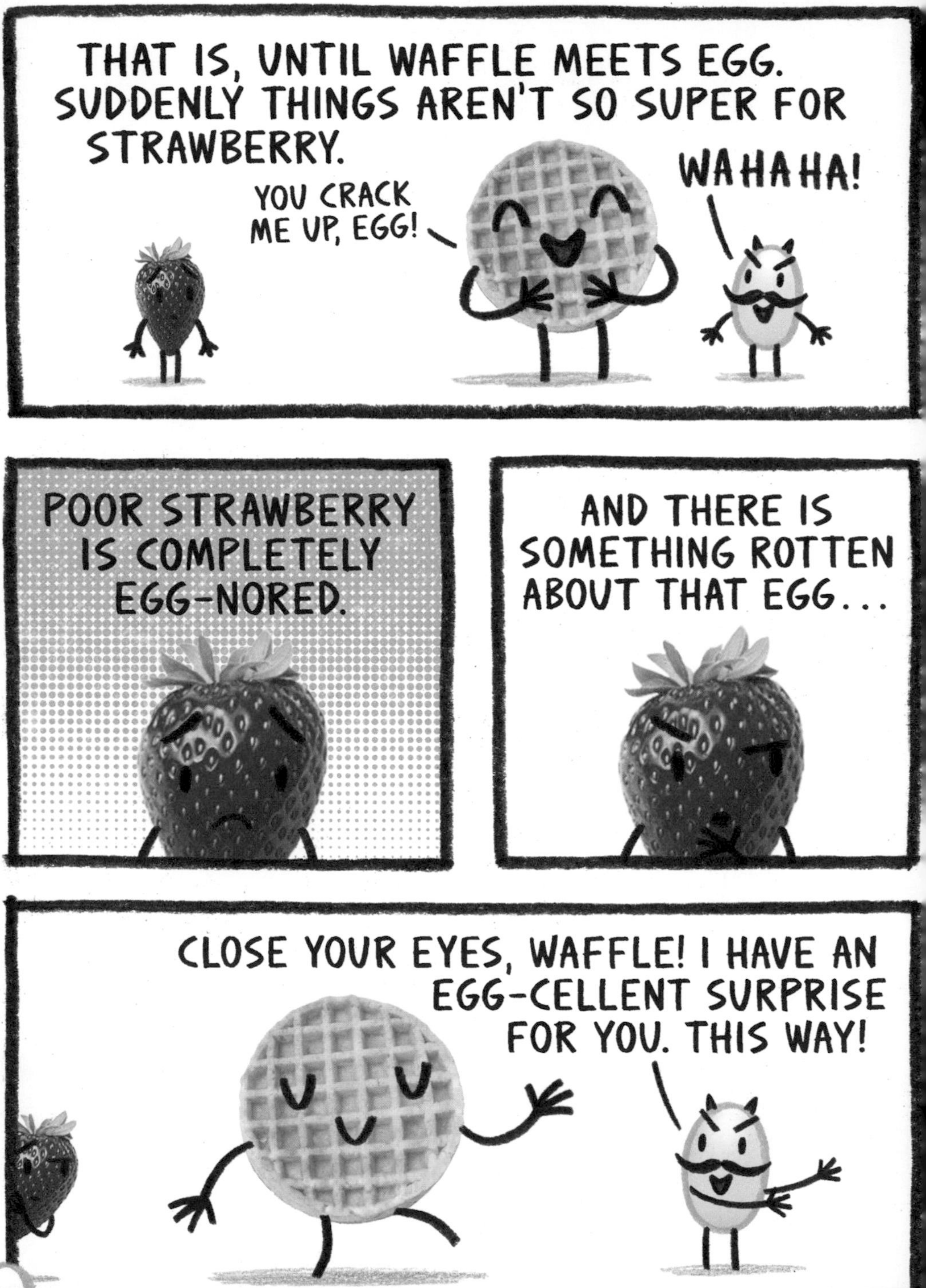
THAT IS, UNTIL WAFFLE MEETS EGG. SUDDENLY THINGS AREN'T SO SUPER FOR STRAWBERRY.
YOU CRACK ME UP, EGG!
WAHAHA!
POOR STRAWBERRY IS COMPLETELY EGG-NORED.
AND THERE IS SOMETHING ROTTEN ABOUT THAT EGG...
CLOSE YOUR EYES, WAFFLE! I HAVE AN EGG-CELLENT SURPRISE FOR YOU. THIS WAY!

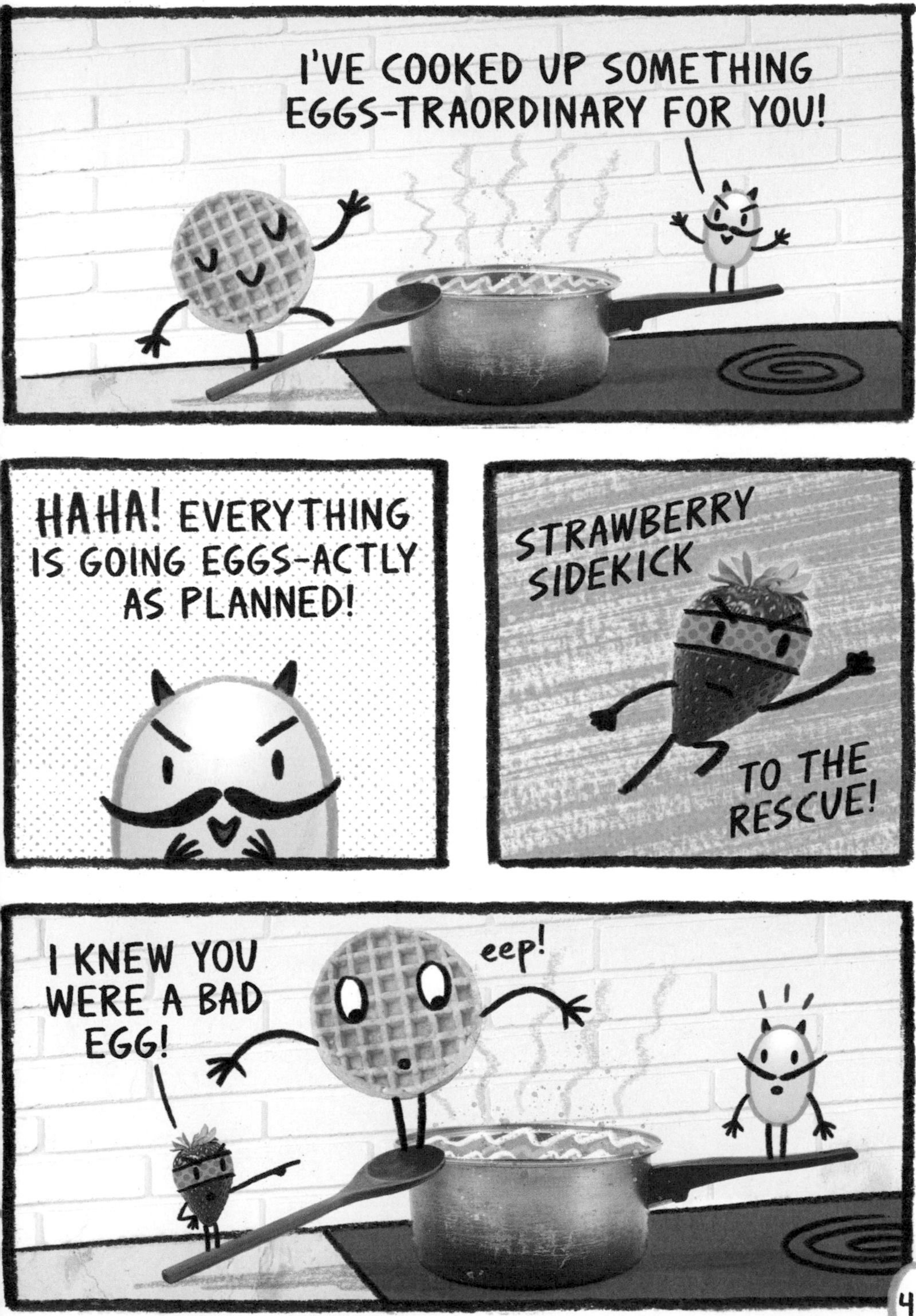
I'VE COOKED UP SOMETHING EGGS-TRAORDINARY FOR YOU!
HAHA! EVERYTHING IS GOING EGGS-ACTLY AS PLANNED!
STRAWBERRY SIDEKICK
TO THE RESCUE!
I KNEW YOU WERE A BAD EGG!
eep!

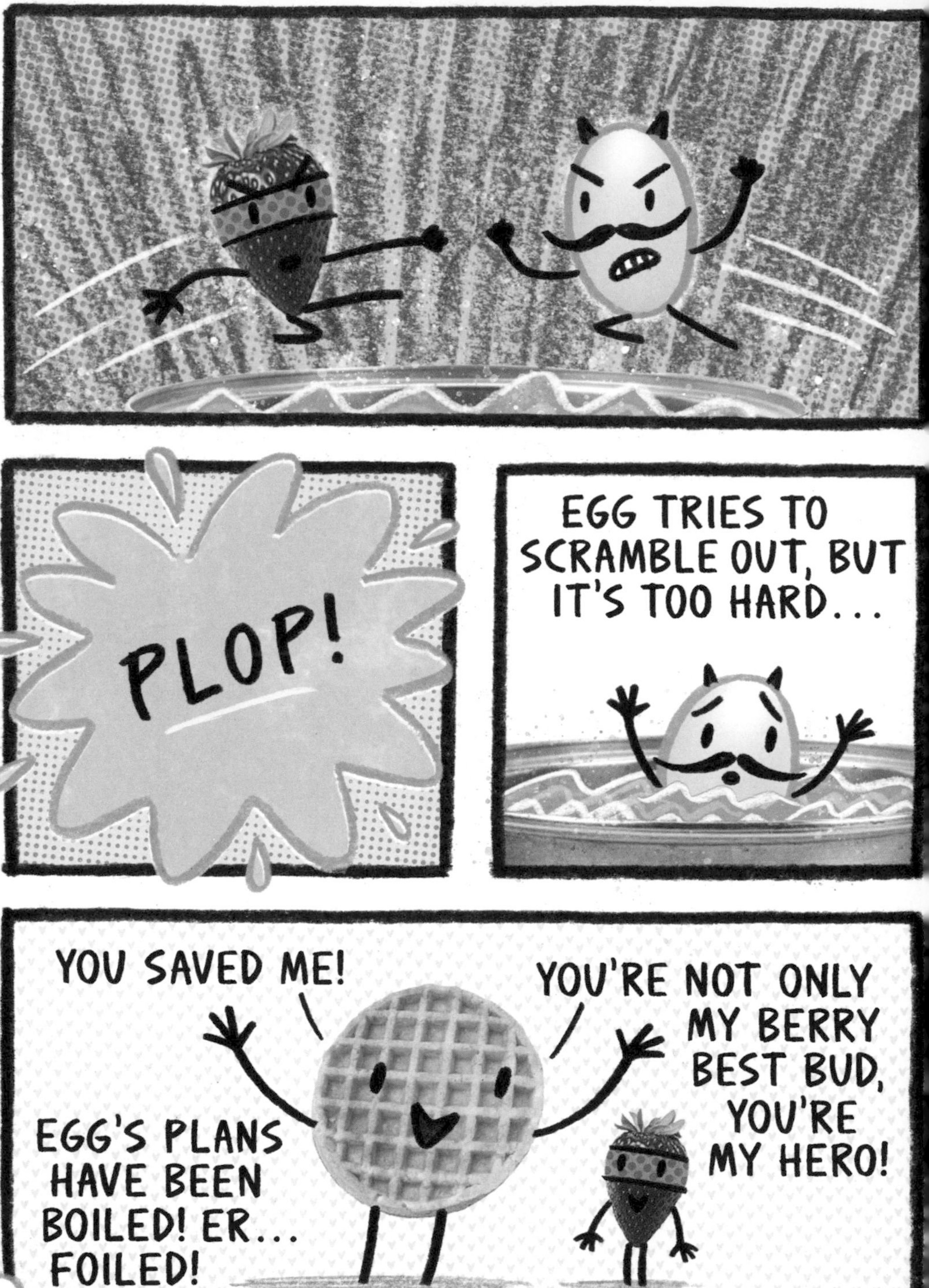
PLOP!
EGG TRIES TO SCRAMBLE OUT, BUT IT'S TOO HARD...
YOU SAVED ME!
YOU'RE NOT ONLY MY BERRY BEST BUD, YOU'RE MY HERO!
EGG'S PLANS HAVE BEEN BOILED! ER... FOILED!

AHOY, ADVENTURE!

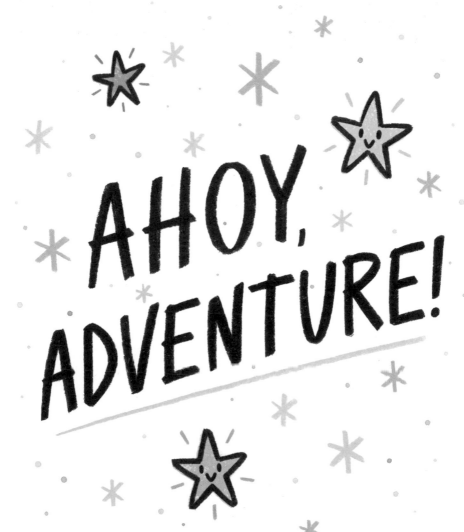

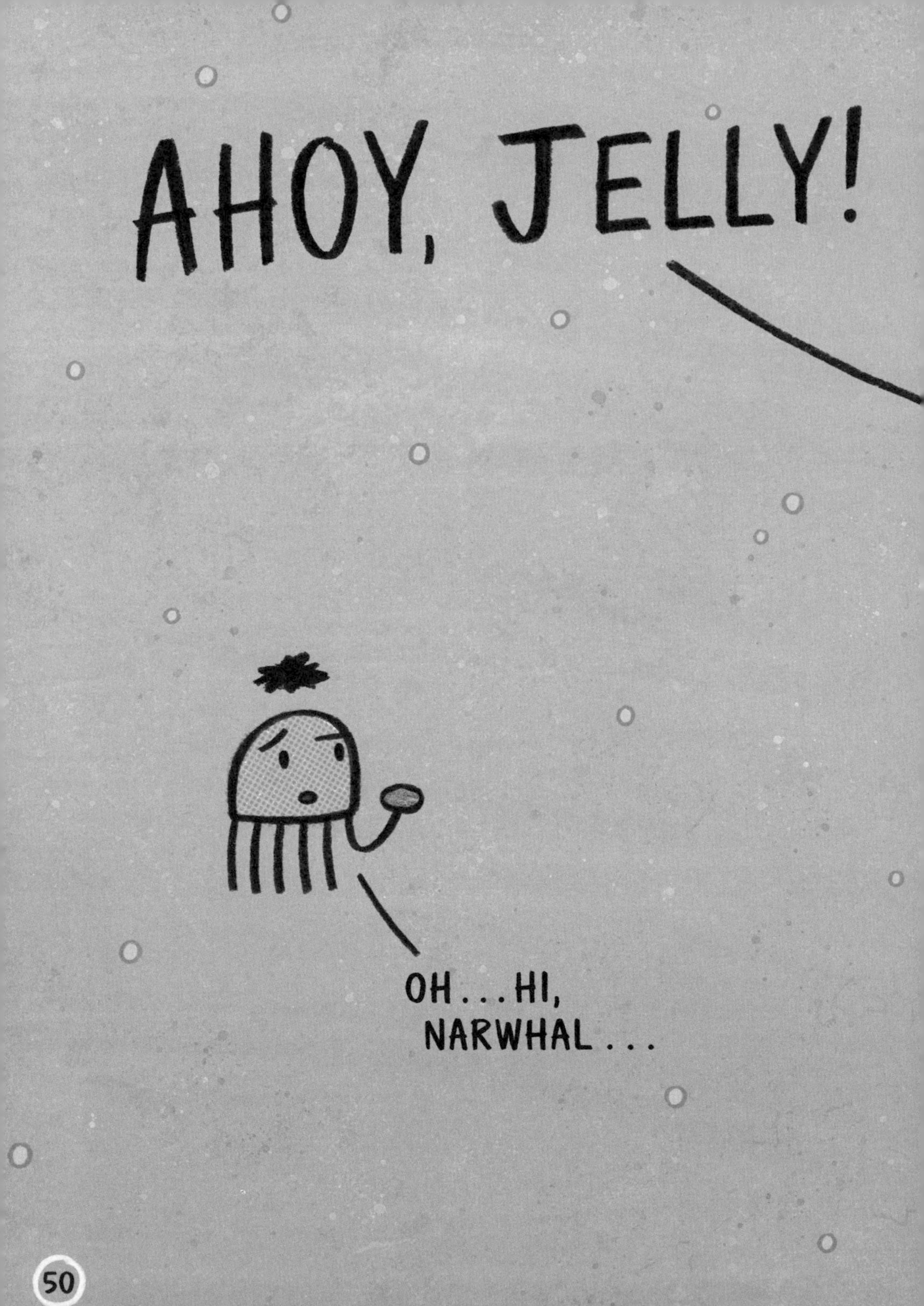
AHOY, JELLY!
OH...HI, NARWHAL...

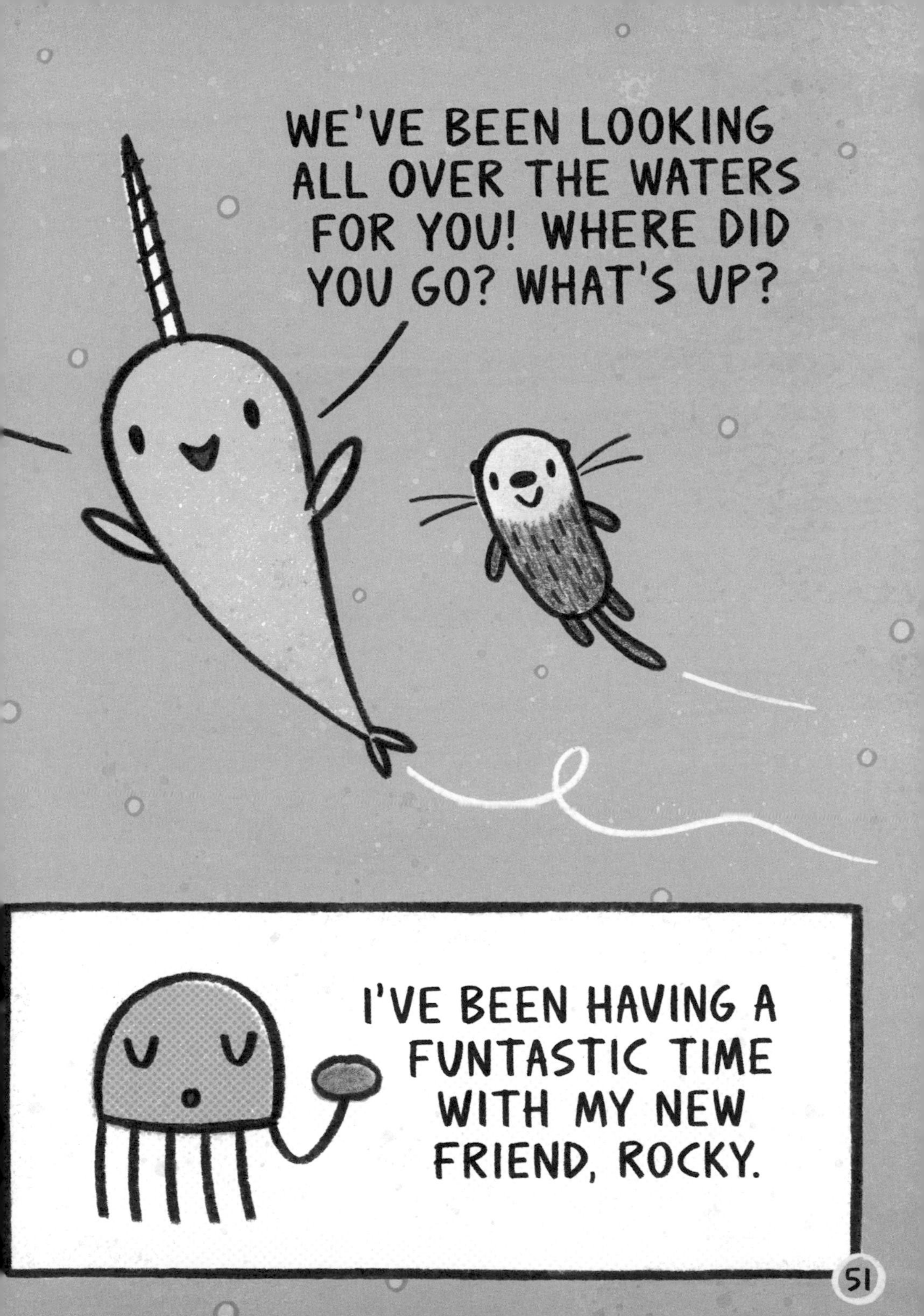
WE'VE BEEN LOOKING ALL OVER THE WATERS FOR YOU! WHERE DID YOU GO? WHAT'S UP?
I'VE BEEN HAVING A FUNTASTIC TIME WITH MY NEW FRIEND, ROCKY.

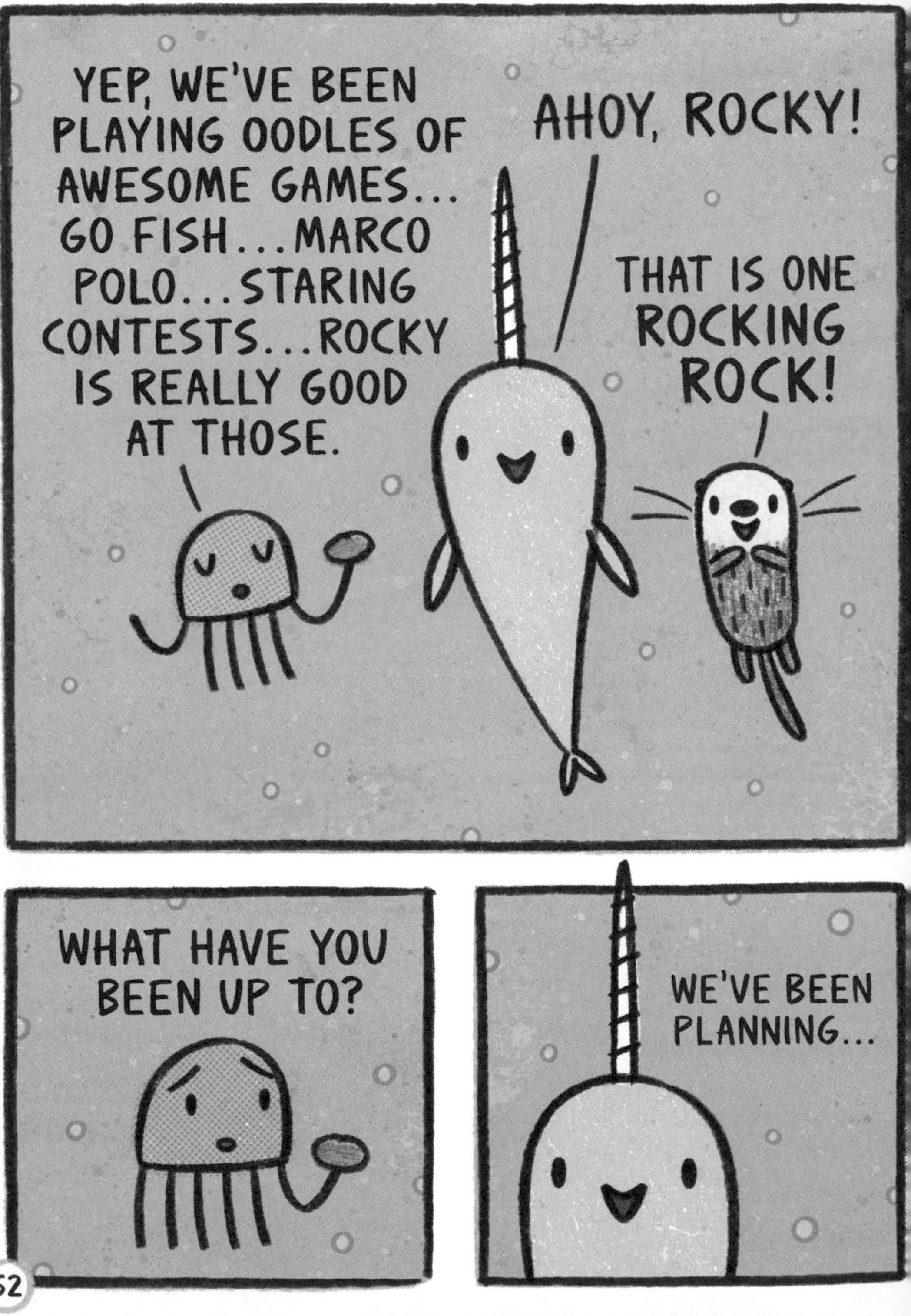

YEP, WE'VE BEEN PLAYING OODLES OF AWESOME GAMES... GO FISH...MARCO POLO...STARING CONTESTS...ROCKY IS REALLY GOOD AT THOSE.
AHOY, ROCKY!
THAT IS ONE ROCKING ROCK!
WHAT HAVE YOU BEEN UP TO?
WE'VE BEEN PLANNING...

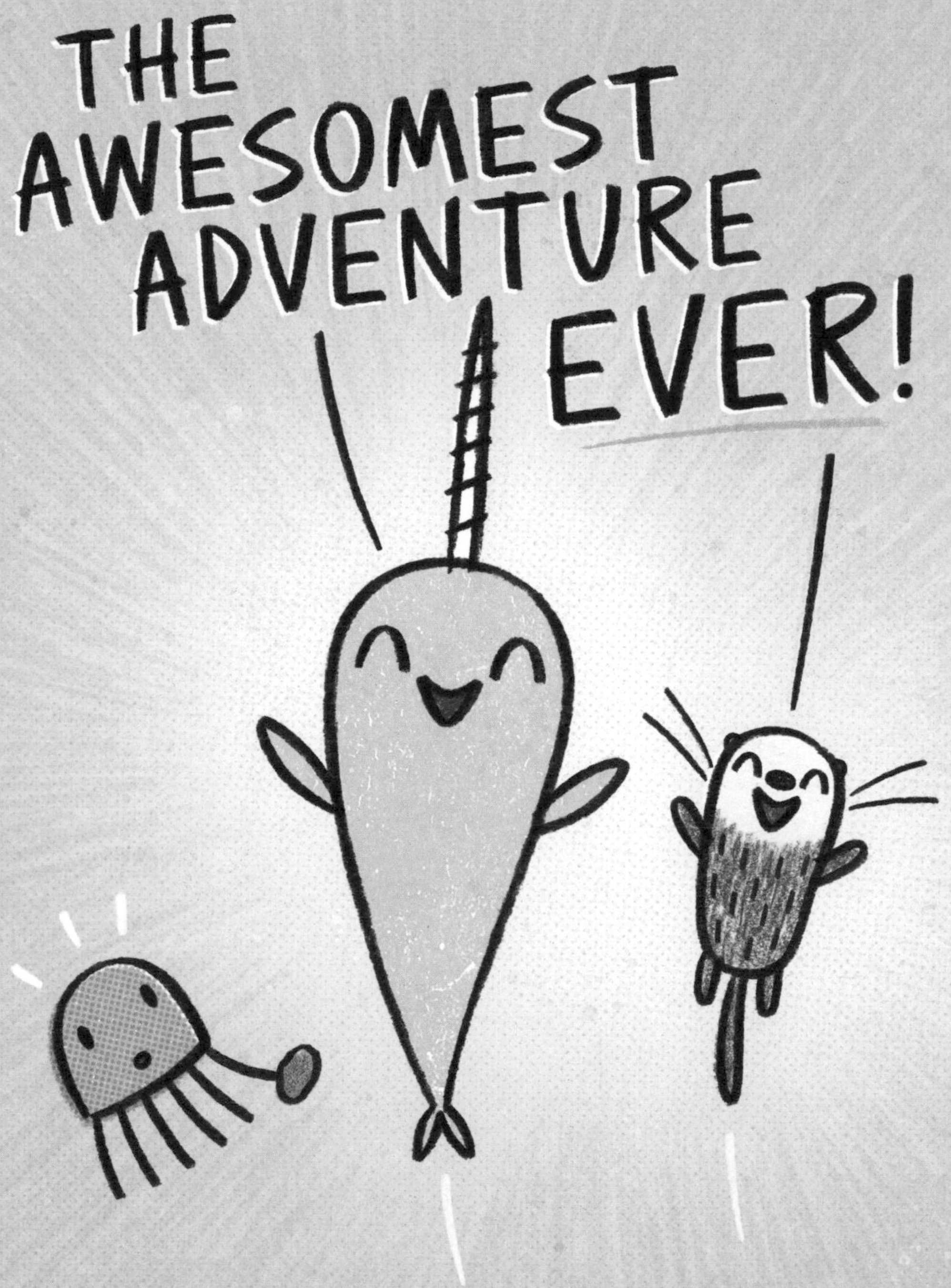
THE AWESOMEST ADVENTURE EVER!

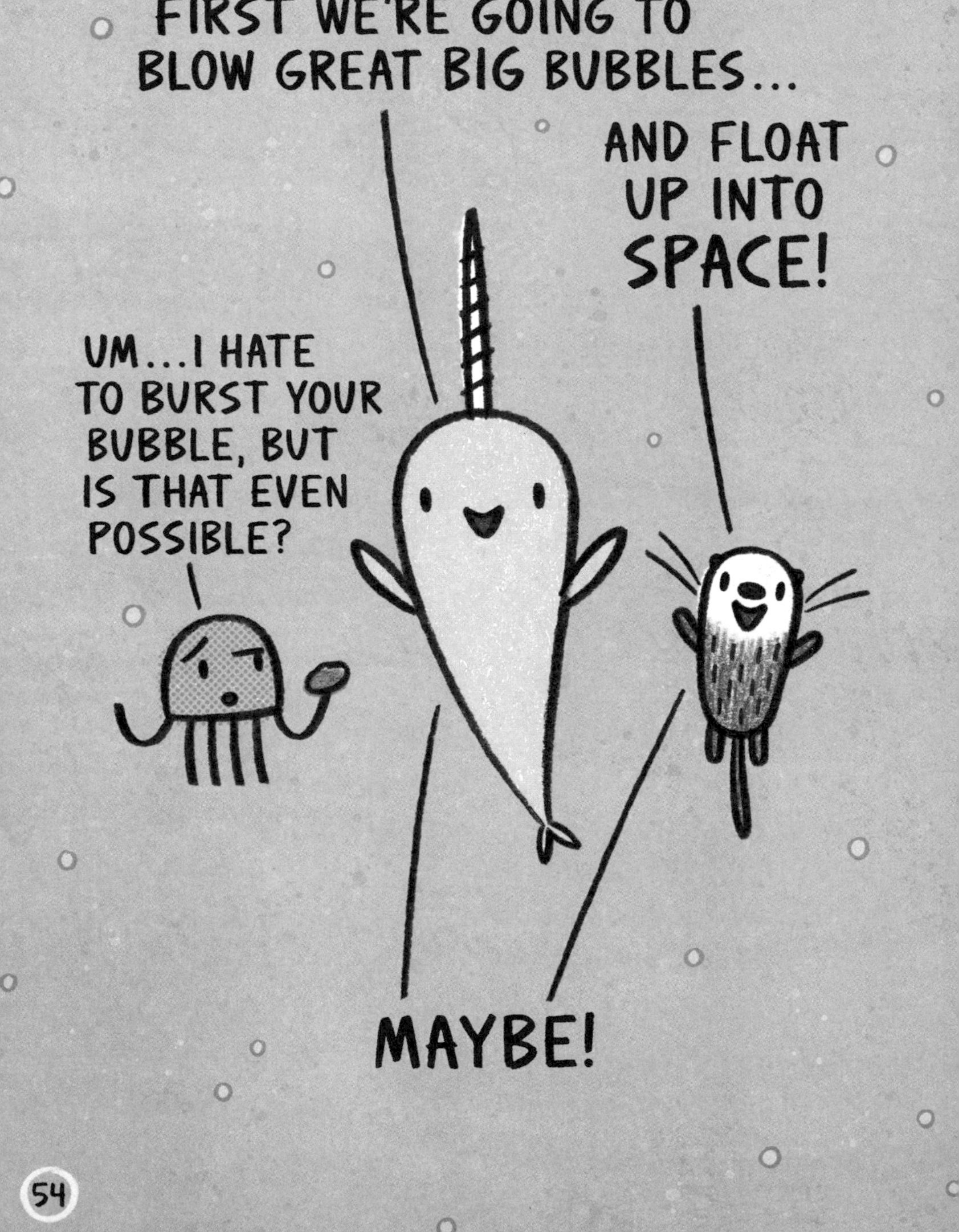
FIRST WE'RE GOING TO BLOW GREAT BIG BUBBLES...
AND FLOAT UP INTO SPACE!
UM...I HATE TO BURST YOUR BUBBLE, BUT IS THAT EVEN POSSIBLE?
MAYBE!

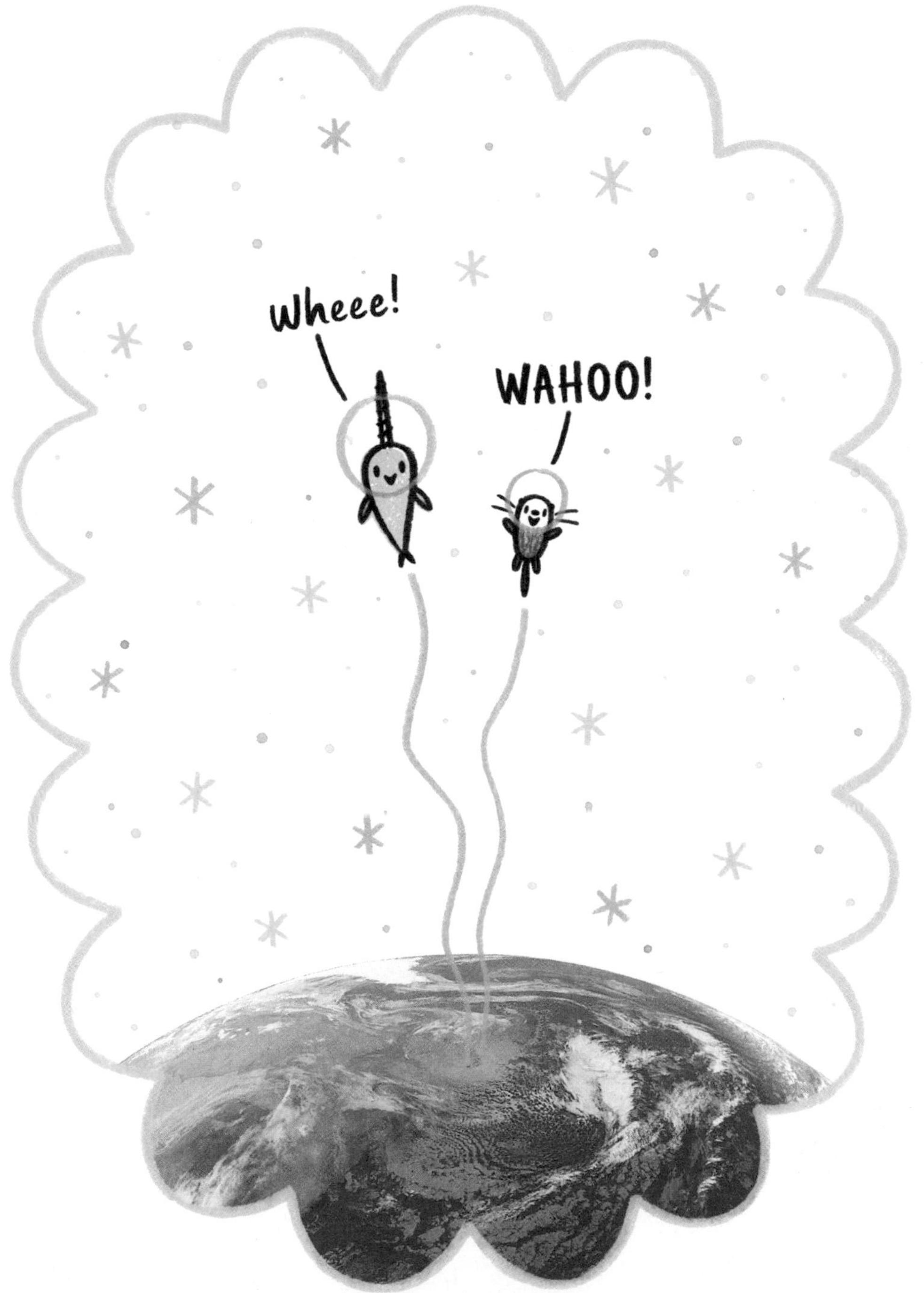
Wheee!
WAHOO!

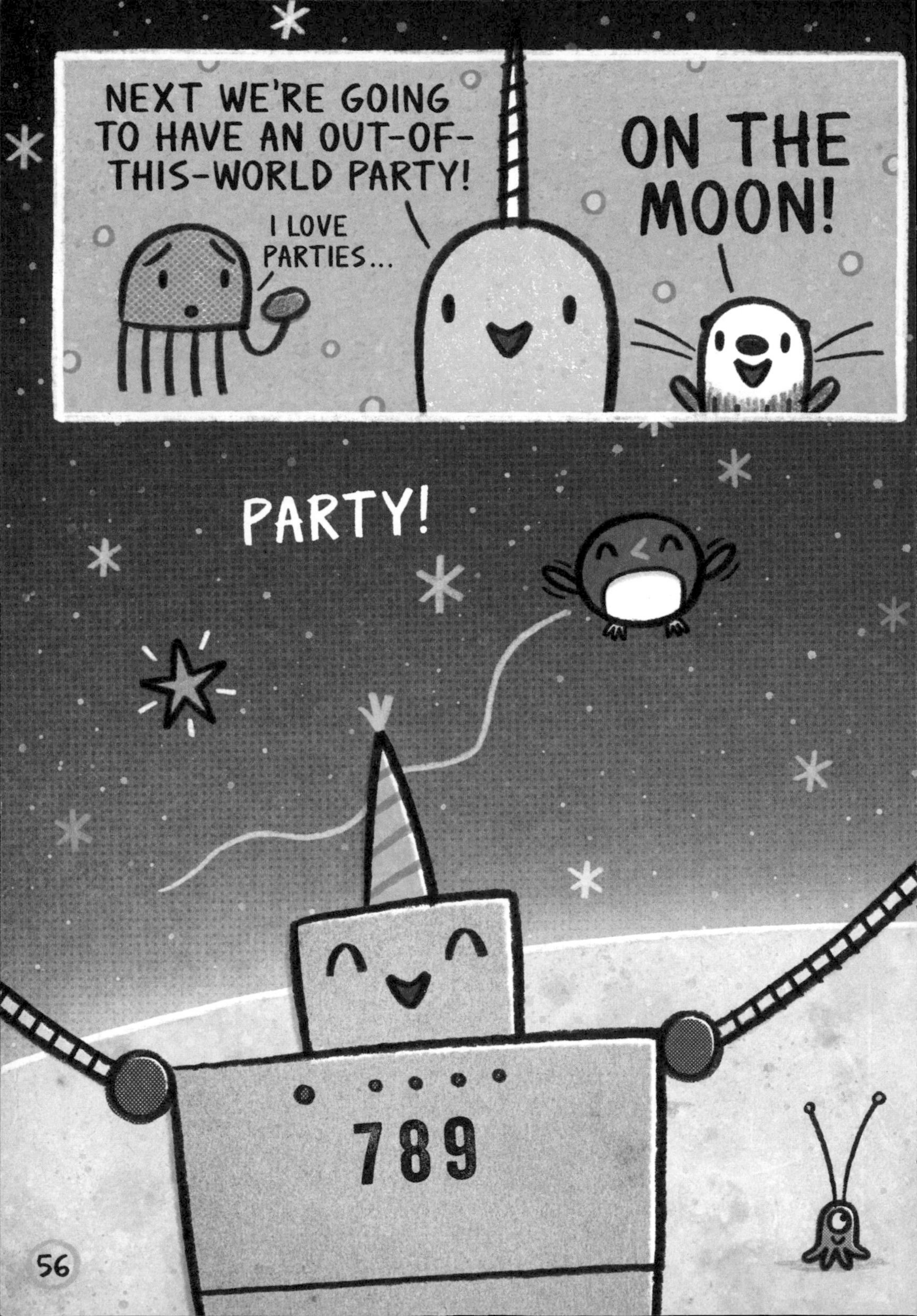
NEXT WE'RE GOING TO HAVE AN OUT-OF-THIS-WORLD PARTY!
I LOVE PARTIES...
ON THE MOON!
PARTY!
789

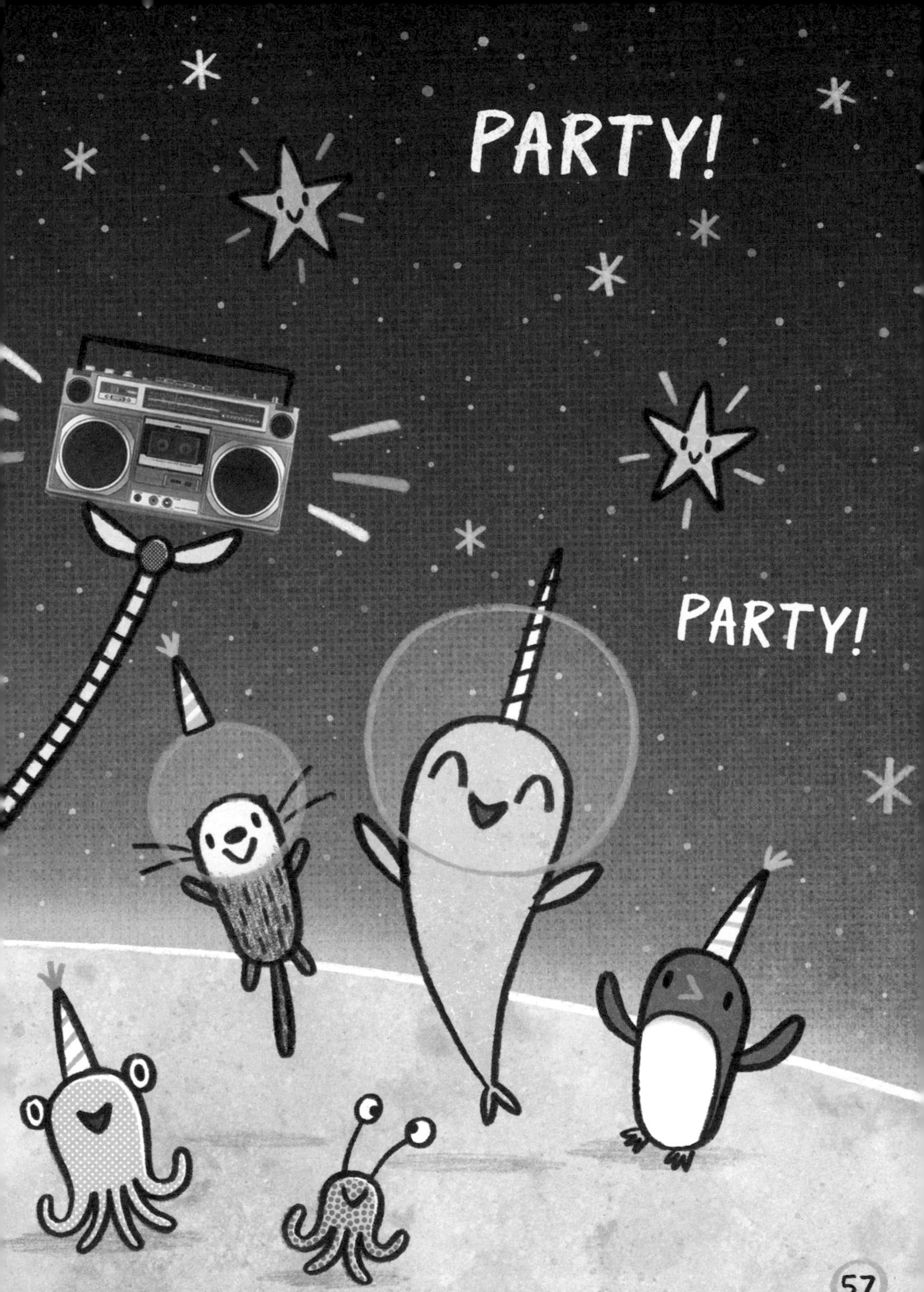
PARTY!
PARTY!

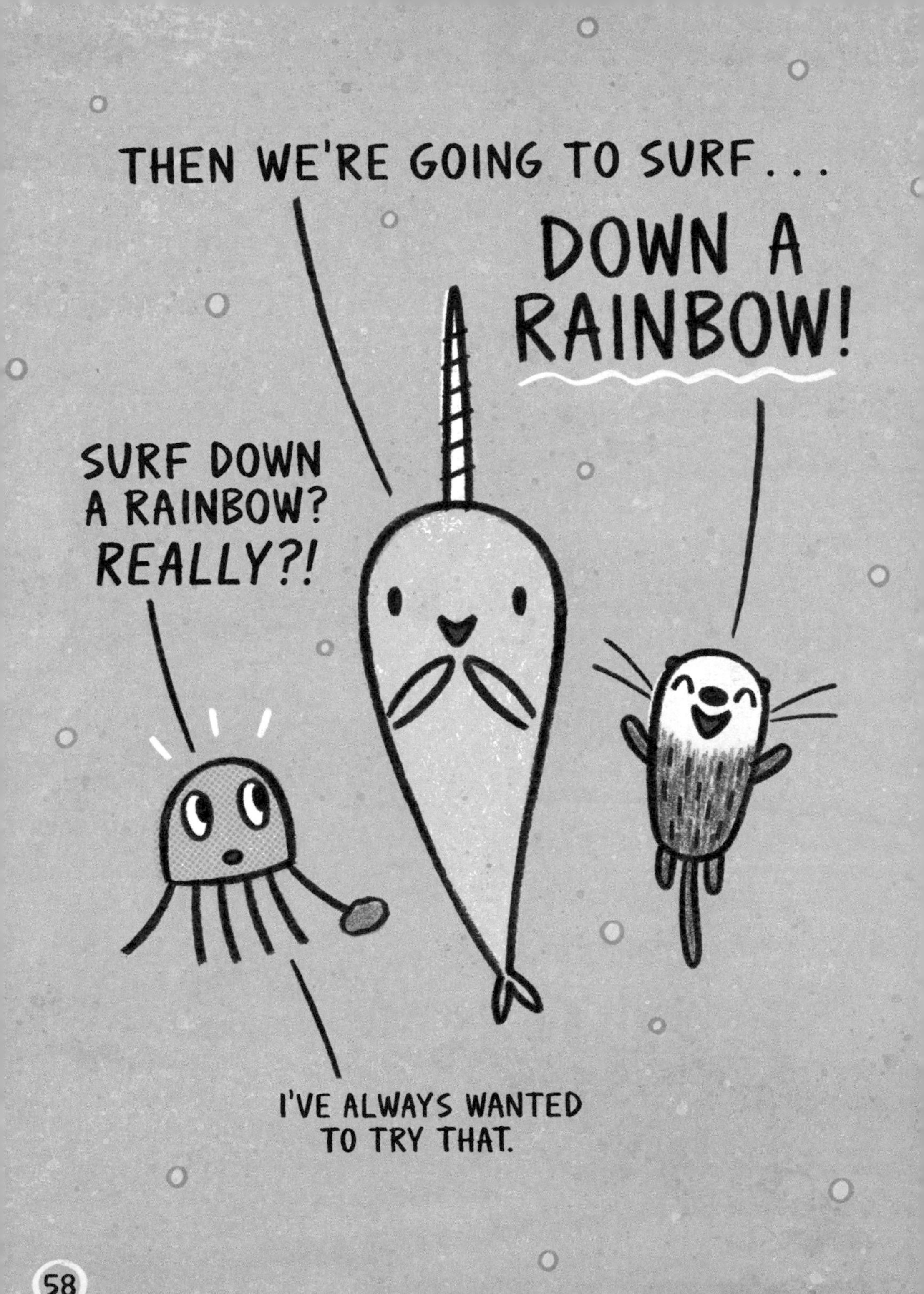
THEN WE'RE GOING TO SURF...
DOWN A RAINBOW!
SURF DOWN A RAINBOW? REALLY?!
I'VE ALWAYS WANTED TO TRY THAT.

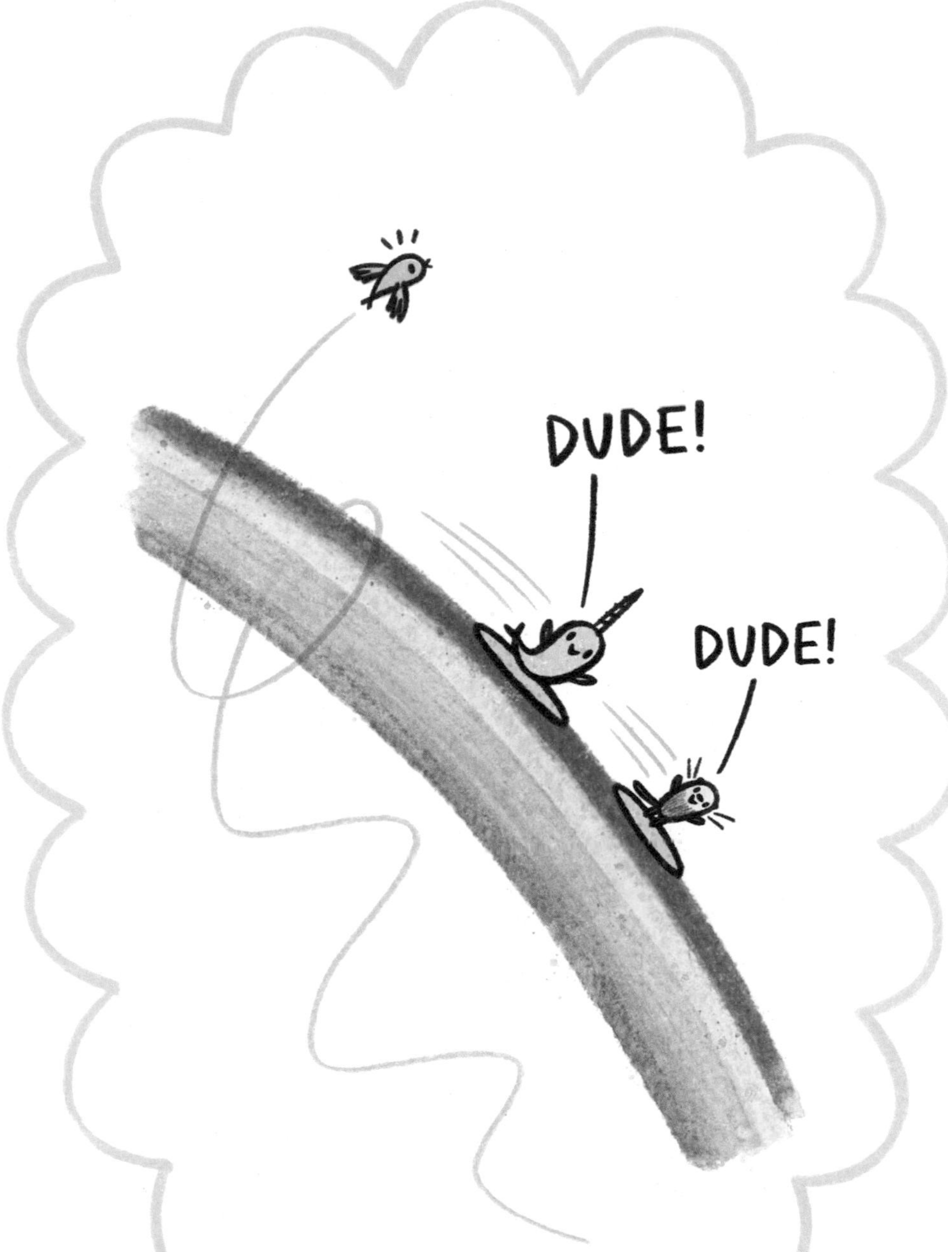
DUDE!
DUDE!

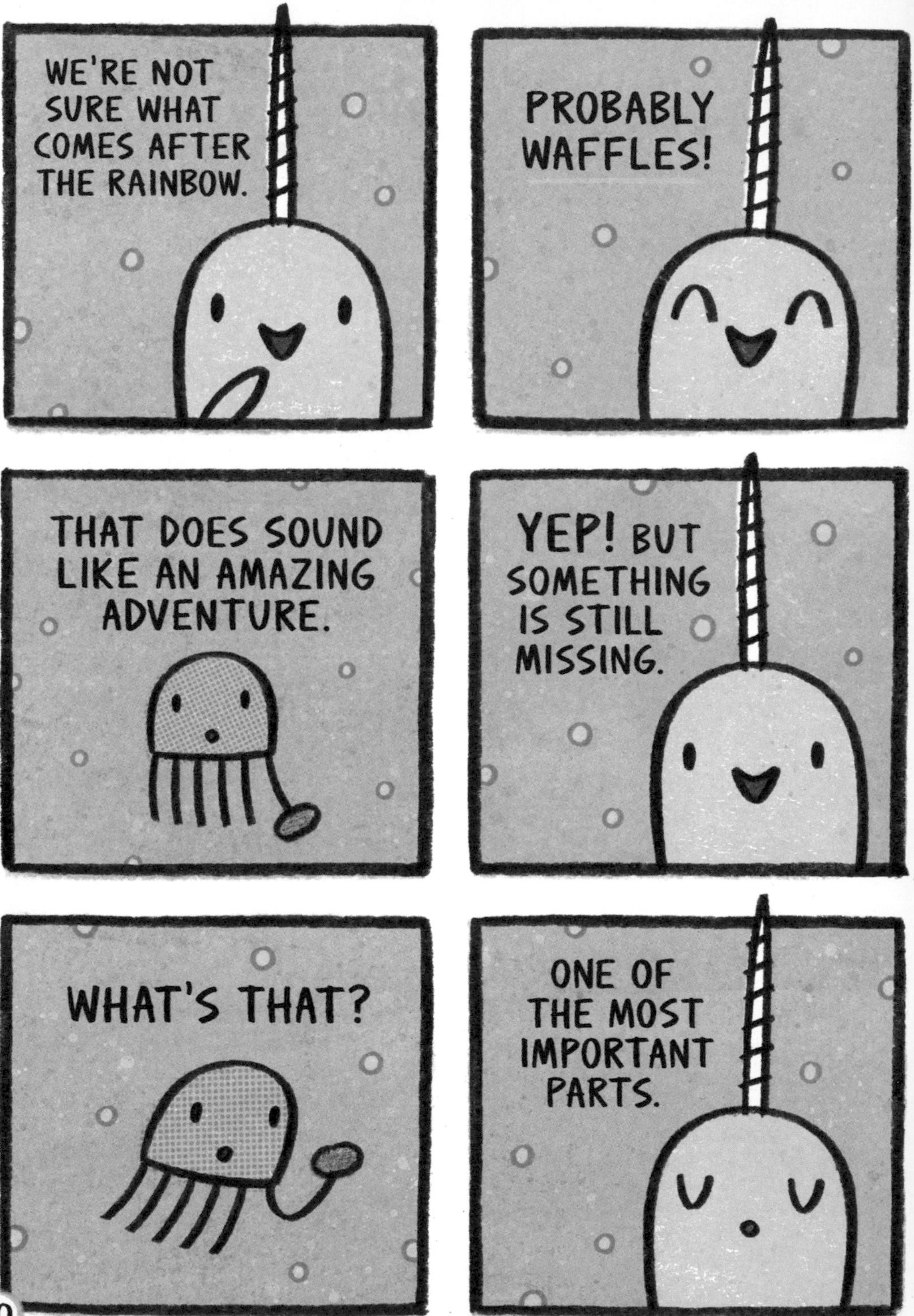
WE'RE NOT SURE WHAT COMES AFTER THE RAINBOW.
PROBABLY WAFFLES!
THAT DOES SOUND LIKE AN AMAZING ADVENTURE.
YEP! BUT SOMETHING IS STILL MISSING.
WHAT'S THAT?
ONE OF THE MOST IMPORTANT PARTS.

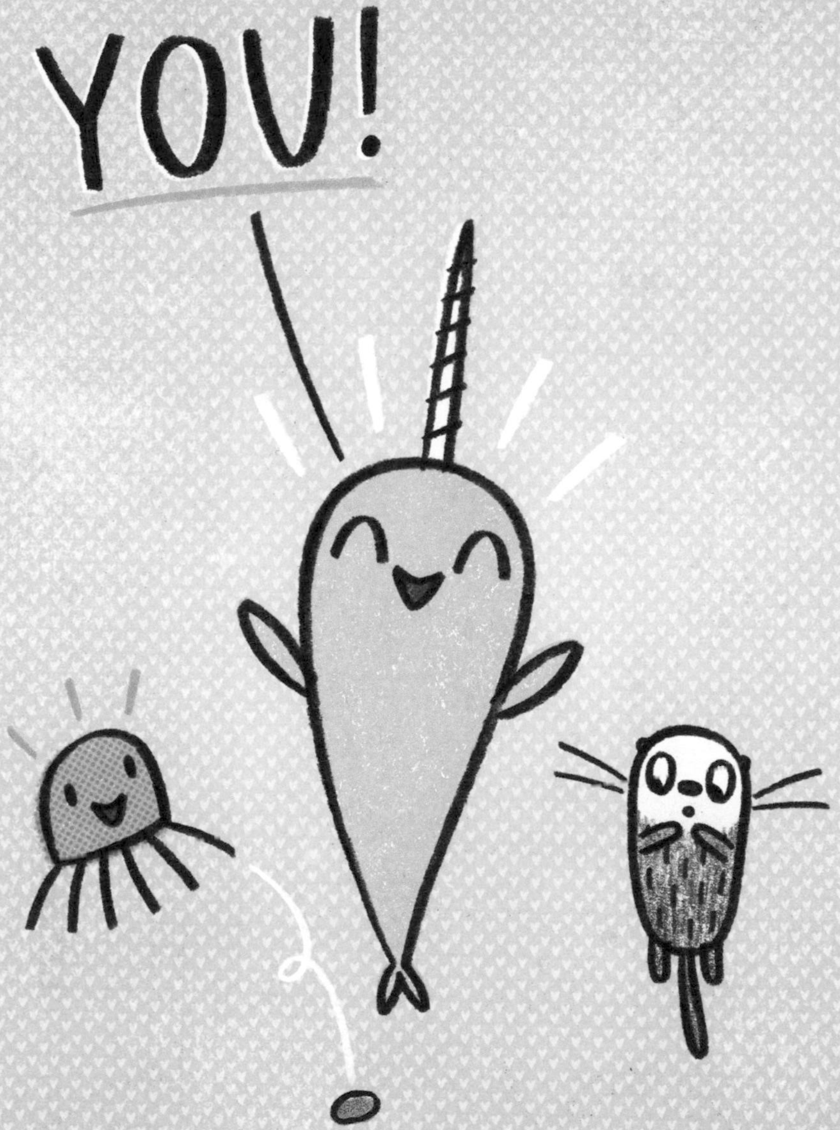
YOU!

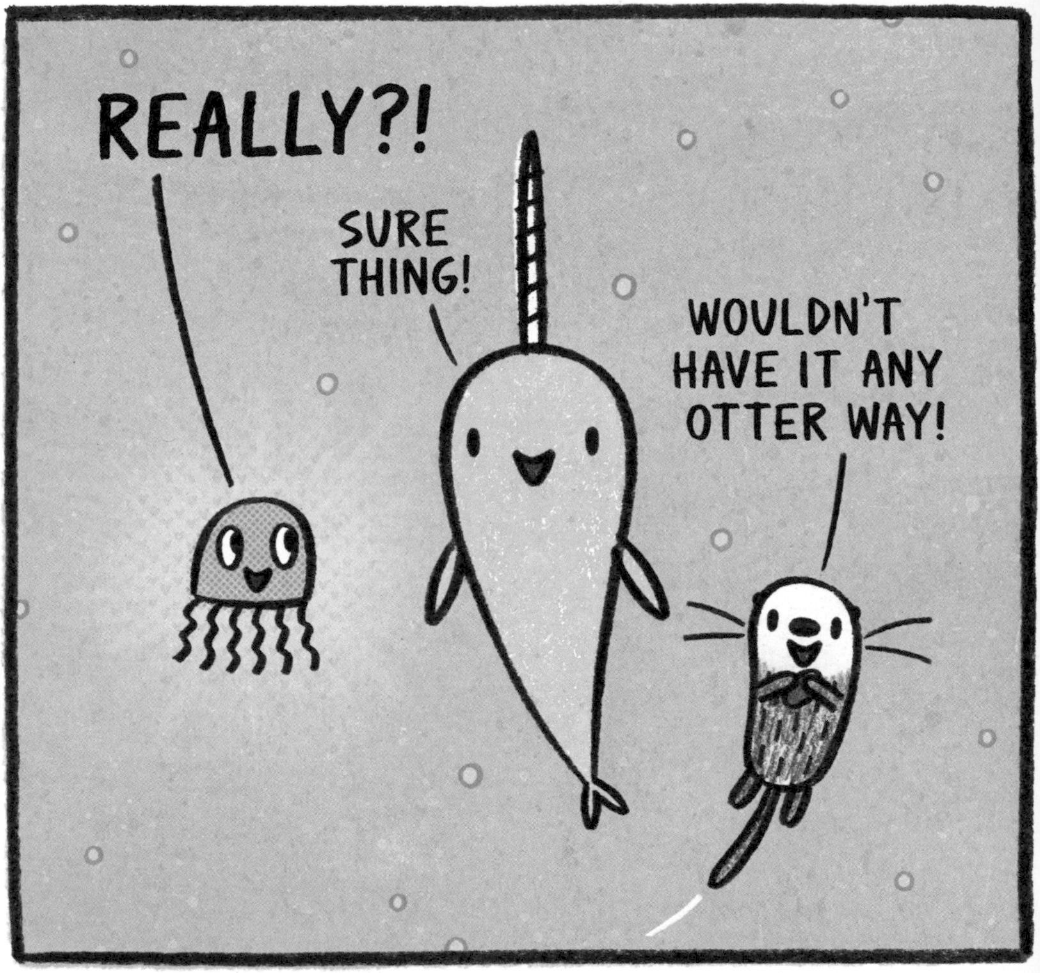
REALLY?!
SURE THING!
WOULDN'T HAVE IT ANY OTTER WAY!

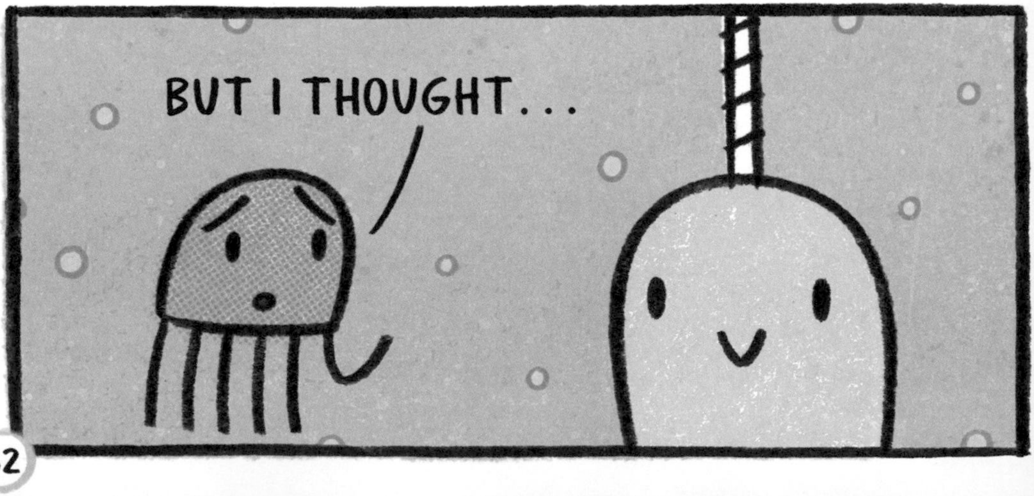
BUT I THOUGHT...

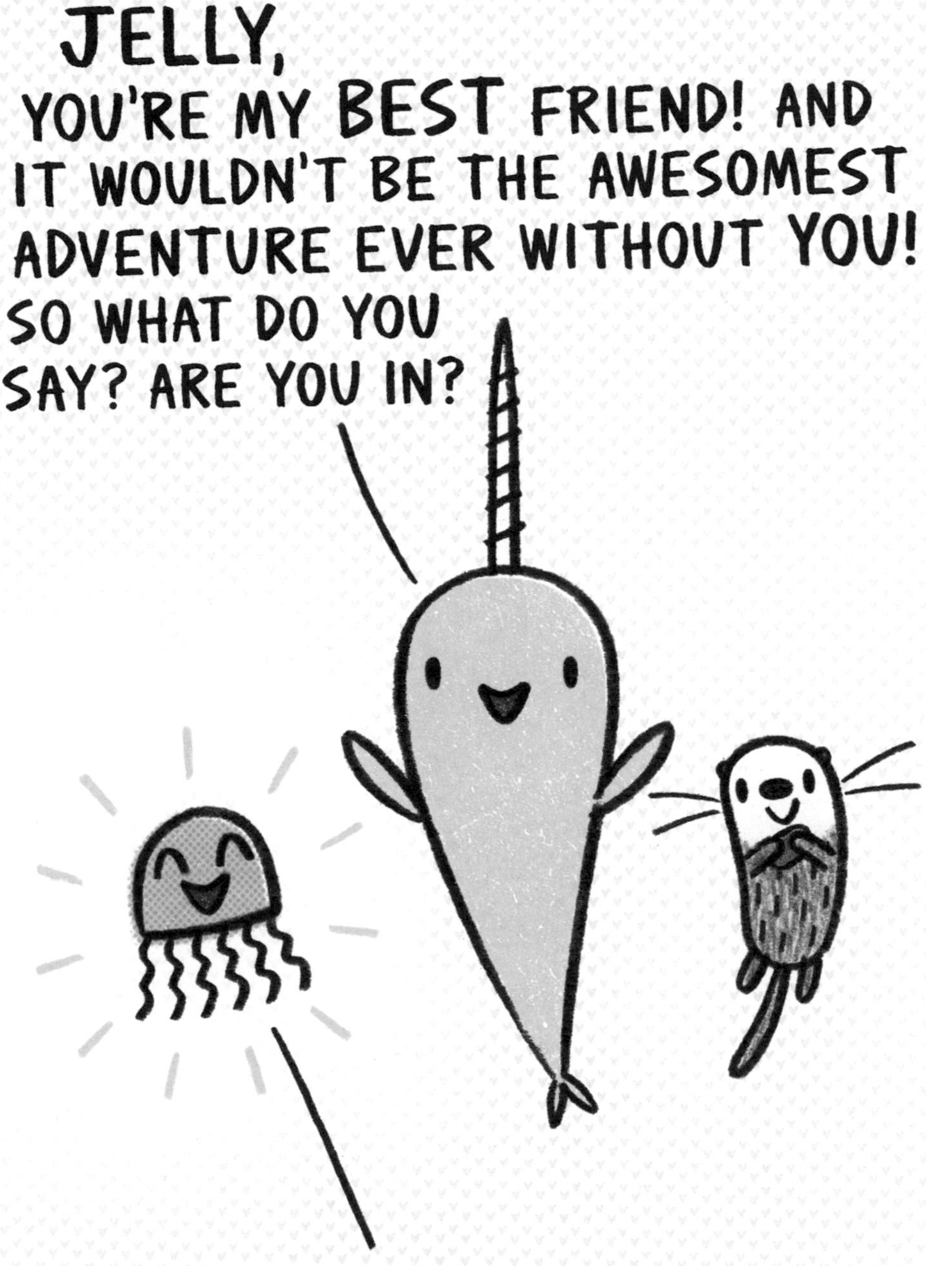
JELLY,
YOU'RE MY BEST FRIEND! AND IT WOULDN'T BE THE AWESOMEST ADVENTURE EVER WITHOUT YOU! SO WHAT DO YOU SAY? ARE YOU IN?
I SAY . . .

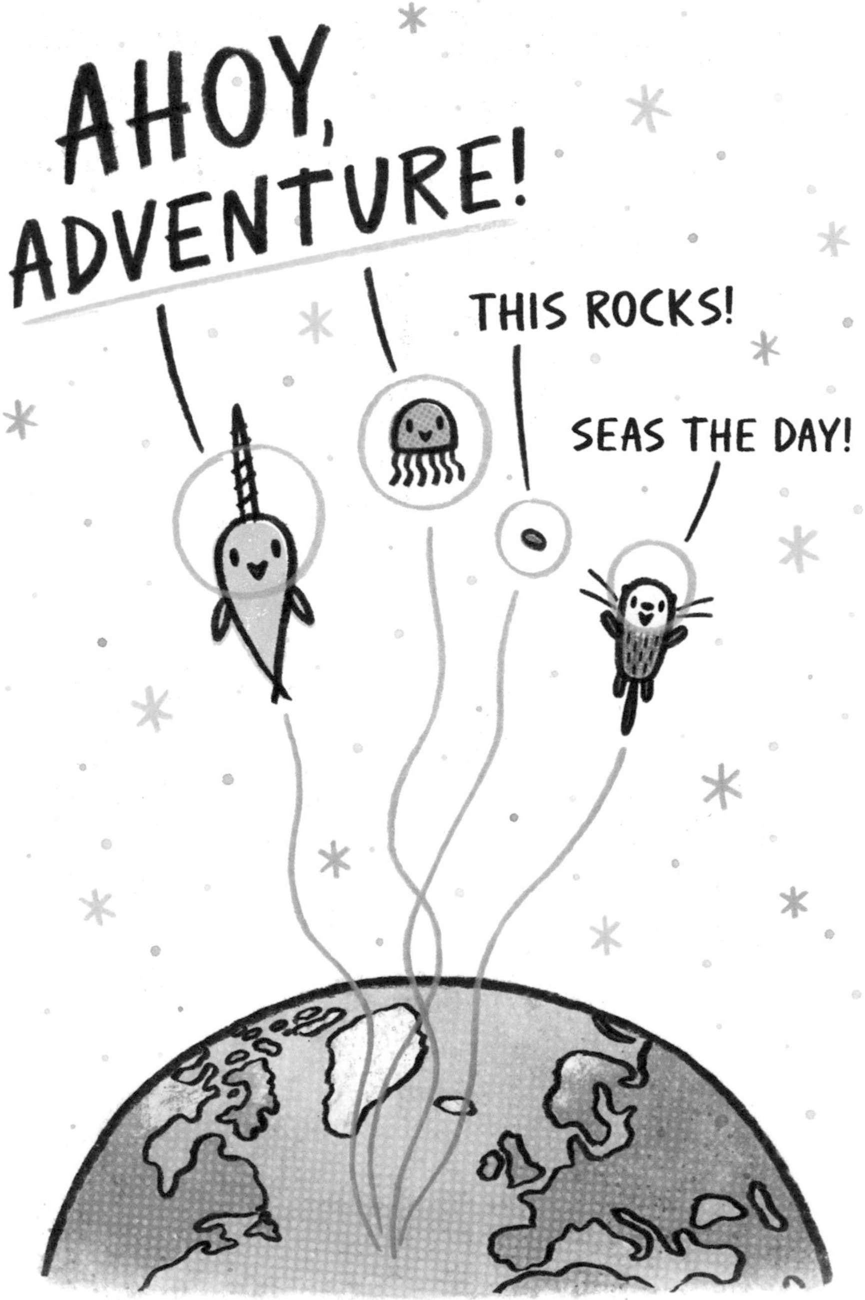
AHOY, ADVENTURE!
THIS ROCKS!
SEAS THE DAY!

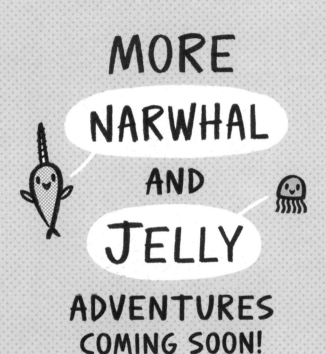

MORE
NARWHAL
AND
JELLY
ADVENTURES
COMING SOON!

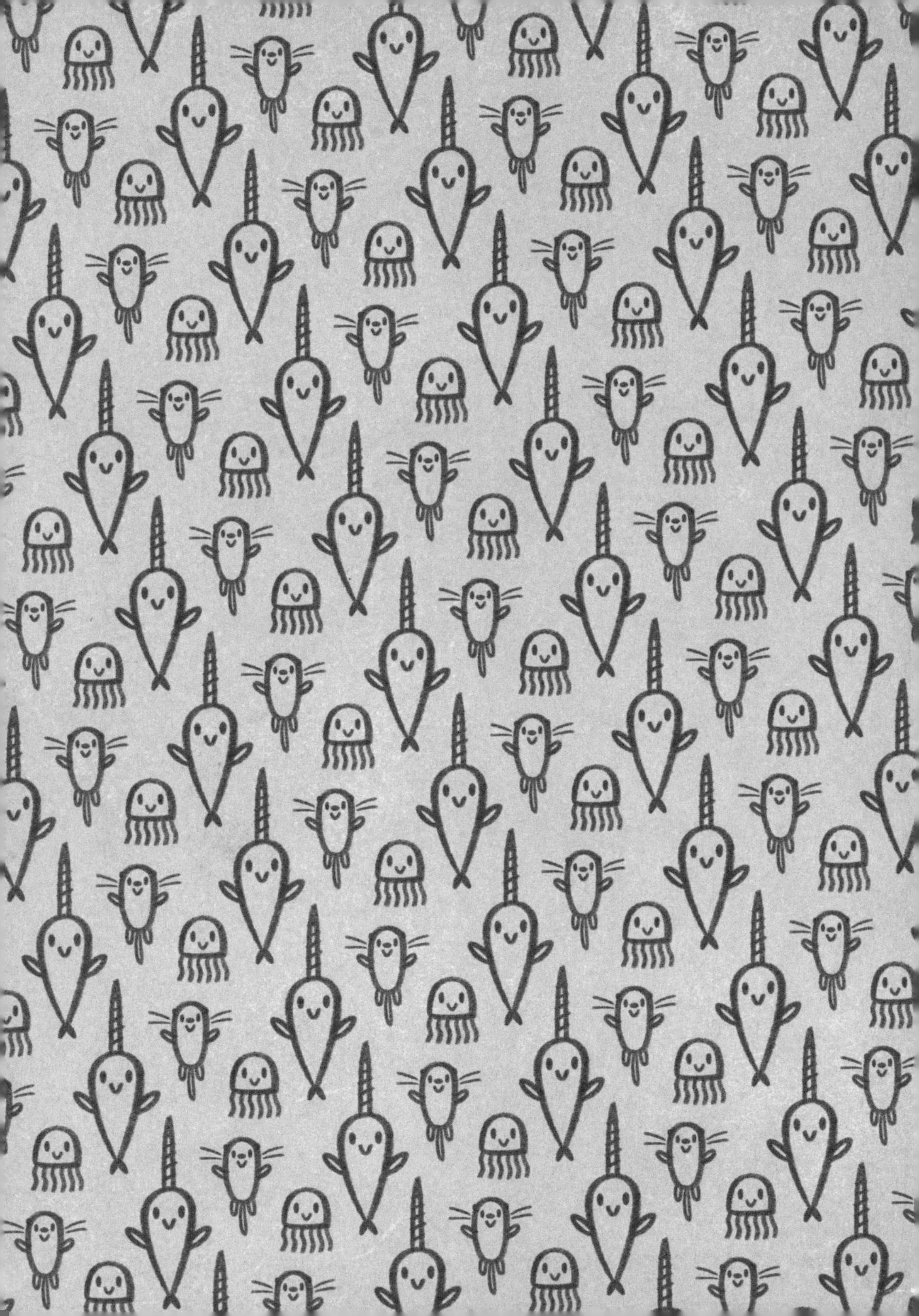